Paul Yoon

LAURA VAN DEN BERG is the author of two story collections, *What the World Will Look Like When All the Water Leaves Us* and *The Isle of Youth*, and the novel *Find Me*. She is the recipient of a Rosenthal Family Foundation Award from the American Academy of Arts and Letters, the Bard Fiction Prize, an O. Henry Award, and a MacDowell Colony fellowship. Born and raised in Florida, she lives in Cambridge, Massachusetts, with her husband and dog.

ALSO BY LAURA VAN DEN BERG

What the World Will Look Like When All the Water Leaves Us

The Isle of Youth

Find Me

Additional Praise for *The Third Hotel*

"Eerily gorgeous . . . Once finished, [the novel] seems to continue beyond the last page, like a dream that stays with you long after waking."
—Natalie Beach, *O, The Oprah Magazine*

"*The Third Hotel* sets a creepy, unsettling mood . . . This is a gorgeous and layered novel that will haunt you for days after you've finished." —Samantha Irby, *Marie Claire*

"*The Third Hotel* contains all of the ingredients for a classic work of horror . . . Not every author can make a character both fly through supernatural events and remain grounded in a place the way Van den Berg does with Clare . . . She's a 'final girl' whose denouement horrifies in a modern, bloodless way." —Bethanne Patrick, *Time*

"Van den Berg doesn't do neatness. She does elegance. She writes with off-kilter beauty and absolute relaxation; the less peaceful a sentence should be, the more peaceful it is."
—Lily Meyer, NPR

"Wonderful, lucid, mysterious."
—James Wood, *Condé Nast Traveler*

"*The Third Hotel* is Van den Berg's second novel and fourth book of fiction, and with it, she has firmly established herself as one of this country's premier stylists . . . Masterful."
—Nick White, *Chicago Review of Books*

"*The Third Hotel* will play tricks on you—and that's the point . . . It's *Twin Peaks* meets literary fiction."

—Elena Nicolaou, *Refinery29*

"Enter *The Third Hotel* like a portal, and surrender to a surreal, vivid, impossible yet clearly realistic adventure . . . Van den Berg uses cinematic language, imagery, and structure in this impressionistic portrait of a marriage that has come undone, a woman whose reality is skewed, and a sea-swept island filled with seductive art, strange vistas, and unexpected danger."

—Jane Ciabattari, BBC Culture

"Beautiful and unsettling . . . Julio Cortázar could see himself walking the partially erased and re-inscribed streets of Van den Berg's imagination, but in the end those streets are, without a doubt, Van den Berg's own."

—Christian Kiefer, *The Paris Review* (staff pick)

"*The Third Hotel* is dense with everything that makes a novel memorable: psychological complexity, sensory vividness, narrative tension, and ideas about humanity and art."

—Claire Fallon, *HuffPost*

"Though subtly drawn, what it means to be a woman becomes just as central to *The Third Hotel* as the mystery of Richard's reappearance. Powerful and atmospheric, Van den Berg's novel portrays a haunting descent into grief and the mysteries we can't quite solve while advancing a thought-provoking exploration of marriage, misogyny, and the loneliness that lurks within unwavering privacy."

—Lauren Sarazen, *Los Angeles Review of Books*

THE THIRD HOTEL

LAURA VAN DEN BERG

PICADOR   FARRAR, STRAUS AND GIROUX   NEW YORK

THE THIRD HOTEL. Copyright © 2018 by Laura van den Berg. All rights reserved. Printed in the United States of America. For information, address Picador, 120 Broadway, New York, N.Y. 10271.

picadorusa.com • instagram.com/picador
twitter.com/picadorusa • facebook.com/picadorusa

Picador® is a U.S. registered trademark and is used by Macmillan Publishing Group, LLC, under license from Pan Books Limited.

For book club information, please visit facebook.com/picadorbookclub or email marketing@picadorusa.com.

Designed by Abby Kagan

Interior art: leaf pattern by greattekat / Shutterstock.com; hand-drawn illustrations by Sarahmay Wilkinson

The Library of Congress has cataloged the Farrar, Straus and Giroux edition as follows:

Names: Van den Berg, Laura, author
Title: The third hotel / Laura, van den berg.
Description: First edition. | New York : Farrar, Straus and Giroux, 2018.
Identifiers: LCCN 2017038339 | ISBN 9780374168353 (hardcover) |
ISBN 9780374714970 (ebook)
Classification: LCC PS3622.A58537 T48 2018 DDC 813/.6—dc23
LC record available at https://lccn.loc.gov/2017038339

Picador Paperback ISBN 978-1-250-21488-1

Our books may be purchased in bulk for promotional, educational, or business use. Please contact your local bookseller or the Macmillan Corporate and Premium Sales Department at 1-800-221-7945, extension 5442, or by email at MacmillanSpecialMarkets@macmillan.com.

First published by Farrar, Straus and Giroux

First Picador Edition: August 2019

10 9 8 7 6 5 4 3 2 1

For Paul,
Always

I raised the camera, pretended to study a focus which did not include them, waited and watched closely, sure that I would finally catch the revealing expression, one that would sum it all up, life that is rhythmed by movement but which a stiff image destroys, taking time in cross section, if we do not choose the essential imperceptible fraction of it.

—Julio Cortázar

I want this epitaph engraved on my tombstone: "See you soon."

—Édouard Levé

PART 1

THE FINGERNAIL

Havana, 2015

What was she doing in Havana?

A simple question and yet she could not find a simple answer. She imagined bumping into someone she had known in upstate New York, in her former life. She would see this person taking photos in the Plaza de la Catedral or on the Paseo del Prado. They would look up from their cameras. They would call her name and wave. They would make remarks about coincidences, about the world being a very small place, and when the inevitable question came—What was she doing in Havana?—she would have no idea how to explain herself.

She might have said,

I am not who you think I am.

She might have said,

I am experiencing a dislocation of reality.

She had come to Havana for the annual Festival of New Latin American Cinema. She had come to meet the director of the first horror film ever to be made in Cuba. She had come to do the things her husband had planned on doing himself but was in no position to do any longer. The official festival hotel stood tall in Vedado. An oval driveway, ringed with royal palms, led visitors to the entrance; in the back, a grand terrace presided over the sea. The hotel was a landmark, positioned on a knoll, the spires visible from even a great distance. Her own hotel was located on a sloped street near the university. She had taken to calling it the Third Hotel because in the airport taxi she had misstated the address, been dropped in the wrong neighborhood, and pleaded with the concierges at two different hotels for directions to her intended destination.

In the lobby of the festival hotel, a mural of a forest spanned the length of a wall. On her first night, in the middle of a reception, she found herself standing in front of that mural. She peered into the shadows, imagined the secrets living in there. She rubbed the green leaves. The paint was smooth, the treetops tinged with gold. She licked a tree and tasted chalk, feeling wild.

How many drinks? asked the festival rep who escorted her out of the lobby and into the night, his Spanish sharp with disdain. He was a young man in a sand-colored blazer, slightly too large in the shoulders, and a white T-shirt printed with the festival logo, a laminated badge beating softly against his chest. She noticed the fine hairs on his upper lip, the soft swell of his earlobes.

Siete. Outside the streets were shadowed, the air lush with heat.

What's your name? he asked. Where are you staying?

Her body remained rooted to the sidewalk, but already her mind was slouching down the sea-dark streets, past the Wi-Fi park, a concrete half circle where people sat hunched in the shadows and tapped away at phones, back into the Third Hotel, and up the steep staircase. The front desk was overseen by a woman in her twenties named Isa. When she checked in, Isa had recorded her name and passport number in a black ledger, her penmanship immaculate; each letter reminded Clare of a miniature house. Isa had warned her to never use the elevator—the last time a guest had tried, the doors got stuck and had to be pried open with meat hooks. Clare was on the fifth floor, the rooms arranged in an oval around a spiraling metal staircase that led to the rooftop. Potted plants sat at the foot of the stairs, green faces tipped upward like subjects awaiting benediction. After a cursory examination of the elevator, Clare suspected the vertical jacks needed replacing. For years it had been her job to notice such details, and now, in Havana, vacation days were flying like birds from her hands.

Seven, she said again. Her palms were sweating. Her teeth ached.

Here she had given everyone who asked a different name. Laurie, Ripley, Sidney. She had claimed to be a film critic for a newspaper. She could walk around an imposter and who would be able to tell otherwise; this was the seduction of traveling unaccompanied. No one had asked her age, but if they did she would have told them the truth, thirty-seven. She understood that some women would want to do the opposite: actual name, fake age.

My name is Arlo, the young man said. I'm a documentarian and you're lucky you're not being filmed right now.

Her real name was Clare. She had never been to Havana before, and when she stepped off the airplane and onto the tarmac, on the second day of December, in a state of delirium that made every surface look like it had just started to melt, a hot wind nearly pushed her to the ground.

None of this was the part that would have been difficult to explain.

Two flights to reach Havana, the second on a very small plane. On the descent she had expected to see the ocean flapping below; instead green fields yawned into the distance, the grass rippled with fog. For two minutes and thirteen seconds, she was convinced the pilot, for no reason that she could understand, was going to crash the plane into the earth, killing them all. She knew how long this feeling lasted because she timed it on her watch.

In Havana, she would see dead streetlights and magnificent boulevards, trees bowing toward each other to form an airstrip of shade; on the pink granite path of the Prado, a man walking two silver huskies in harnesses, shirtless Rollerbladers whipping past the dogs. She would see security cameras with necks that reminded her of white cranes and a neighborhood library with a sign that read MUERTE AL INVASOR and a dachshund chained to a stool, in the olive attire of a revolutionary. The city was an entirely different place in the daytime than at night. She found homages to artists of all nationalities—the Bertolt Brecht Cultural Center, a park dedicated to Victor Hugo, a bust of Mozart. She would walk for miles without seeing a grocery but pass a dozen places to buy pizza or fruit or ice cream. Soaring brutalist structures severed blocks of colonial houses, with their arches and columns and balconies. Buildings on the edge of total ruin stood adjacent to hotels with doormen. In Plaza de San Francisco, sunburned families in al fresco cafés, babies howling miserably in high chairs, and a flock of pigeons that didn't fly anywhere—that just circled and circled. In Havana, she would see her husband for the first time in thirty-five days.

She was scheduled to stay for one week. Since the trip had been intended for both of them, everything had been booked for two: two visas purchased online; an empty seat next to her on the flights; two sheets of tickets for the films. She kept the spare items in a drawer in her room. She told herself she was setting them aside for a person who had yet to arrive.

On her first day at the festival, she wandered the conference rooms housing press events, savagely hungover, surrounded by people with laminated badges, people who looked like they knew what they were doing. The director she sought was named Yuniel Mata. For him, she had a list of questions, written out on the plane. In her hotel room, she had been practicing her greeting in the bathroom mirror. *Hello*, she would say to her reflection, in her very best Spanish. *My husband was a great admirer of what you are doing.* Yuniel Mata's film was called *Revolución Zombi*. He had shot it entirely on digital and entirely in Havana and all for two million dollars—facts her husband, a film studies professor, had found extraordinary. His specialty was horror. She'd always thought this sounded like a made-up job, and when she had too much to drink at parties she shared this thought with their friends. The festival was her husband's world and she had not anticipated it being so difficult to navigate.

On her second day, she attended a press event with Yuniel Mata and two producers in a conference room with chandeliers and bloodred carpeting. A fake Christmas tree stood in a corner, the branches alight with silver balls. She had to concentrate very hard to track the conversation, a terrible pressure gathering in the back of her skull. In college, she spent a semester in Madrid, followed by a disastrous summer stint as a nanny for a moneyed family in Salamanca; her Spanish was still serviceable, though gaps in understanding kept taking her by surprise. Blank spaces would appear where there should have been a word, a thought.

According to the program, the lead actress, Agata Alonso, was scheduled to participate in the panel. Her bio noted that she was Cuban-born, a current resident of Spain, and best known for a recurring role in a popular Spanish telenovela. *Revolución Zombi* was her first feature. The night before, Clare overheard two men talking about how this actress had failed to show up for the opening gala. She was not in her room or answering her phone. No one had said she was missing, but at the same time her whereabouts were not exactly known. Now she was not at the press event and the panel had not accounted for her absence.

Instead they discussed the zombie school they had established to instruct extras in proper lurching and vocalization and makeup. One extra had gotten carried away and started biting shoulders. A podiatrist had found a bloodied shirt in the gutter and called the Committee for the Defense of the Revolution.

On the plane, Clare had been seated next to a film critic from Rio, and she noticed this same critic, Davi, near the front of the conference room, next to Arlo. As they disembarked, Davi had called the sun in Havana prodigious, even in December, and advised her to be careful with the weather. Davi had a compact, athletic build. He wore fashionable glasses. His eyebrows were two perfect dark arches. When she replied that a childhood in Florida had taught her all she needed to know about heat, he'd patted the canvas shell of her backpack, smiled a smile of vague pity, and wished her a good trip.

When a young woman rose, Clare could tell she was nervous to ask her question. She pressed the tip of her pencil to her notepad. Why make a horror film? she asked, her voice faltering slightly on the *why*. Why not make a movie about things that really happen?

The producers looked to Yuniel Mata, who was already leaning forward in his chair, readying his reply. He wore black slacks and a black T-shirt and neon green sneakers, thin rope bracelets on his wrists. Casual yet sharp. His hair was just long enough to be secured in a ponytail, and he was tall and slender, like her husband.

Mata said to plunge a viewer into a state of terror meant to take away their compass, their tools for navigating the world, and to replace it with a compass that told a different kind of truth. The trick was ensuring the viewer was so consumed by fright that they didn't even notice this exchange was being made; it was a secret transaction between their imagination and the film, and when they left the theater, those new truths would go with them, swimming like eels under the skin.

Besides, he added, raising a finger, the foundation of horror is a dislocation of reality, a dislocation designed to reveal the reality that has been there all along, and such dislocations happen all the time.

Afterward Clare waited in a line to speak with the director. When only the nervous young woman stood between them, an assistant in a navy skirtsuit appeared and whisked him away.

That evening brought the inaugural screening of *Revolución Zombi*, at Cine Charlie Chaplin. Clare had traveled over a thousand miles to see this film and yet when she came upon the marquee sign that bore the title a very strange thing happened.

It was as though an invisible wall had sprung up between her and the theater, and she was unable to take a single step closer. Her eyelids fluttered. Her bowels seized. People flowed around her, joined the sprawling entrance line; she was a rock in a river. She backed away, one small movement at a time, retreating into the shadows until the sign left her sight.

In the morning, she woke afraid of meeting that invisible wall again, of what might happen if she did, so she went to the Malecón at sunrise because her husband found meaning in things like sunrises and because the Malecón was where a climactic scene in *Revolución Zombi* had been filmed. Maybe seeing it would take an invisible brick out of that invisible wall.

She went down long, curving streets, under laundry slung over balconies, plastic bags clipped with pink pins to clotheslines. She passed a turquoise Belle Époque mansion, the sagging facade supported by once-magisterial green columns, the pillars now listing under the burden. She peered through a tall window expecting to glimpse ceiling or wallpaper; her eye instead met a patch of sky. The courtyard walls were crumbling. The grass had grown wild. A few blocks down, a pale yellow colonial with a white wrought-iron fence, the paint bright. The yard was a manicured stamp of green, framed by red gingers and birds of paradise. A blue-and-white placard with a symbol that looked like an upside-down anchor was posted above the doorway, indicating that the house was available for rent. At the bottom of the street, a graffitied figure in a black balaclava stretched across a weathered wall, with a signature that read *2 + 2 = 5*.

She lost her way and ended up in a park, by a barren stone fountain sheltered by palm trees, the pointy fronds tilting in the breeze. She came upon an off-duty mime, his clothes and skin and hair all spray-painted gold, sitting on a bench and talking into a small white cell phone. The gilded mime nodded as she passed. The air was still tinged with night.

At the Malecón, the limestone seawall made the city look like a fortress: impenetrable, foreboding. She passed the occasional jogger and a hunched old man pushing a shopping cart filled with butterscotch candy and two younger men fishing beside a sign that read NO PESCAR. Ahead she couldn't see anything beyond the flat gloss of the ocean, and the longer she stayed, the more it looked like the rising sun was setting the water on fire, and so she stood there, in a blaze fierce enough to remind any person that they were never not at the raw mercy of the earth, and waited to be burned up.

Back in the old part of the city, Clare found her husband standing, inexplicably, outside the Museum of the Revolution, a former presidential palace with immense white columns and a bronze tank stationed outside. The museum cast an enormous shadow and her husband was standing within that shadow. She recognized him first from behind, from several hundred feet away, and stopped in the middle of the sidewalk because she was dizzy and her mouth felt like it was packed with rocks. She ordered herself to stop recognizing him, since what she was recognizing was plainly impossible, but then she crept closer and saw just how possible it was. He was wearing a white linen suit she had never seen before, loafers with leather tassels. His neck was craned, a hand pressed to his brow, as though he were tracking something in the sky.

The contrails of an airplane. The flight of a cloud.

Outside the museum, she asked herself if she should hurl her arms around his shoulders and weep? Demand answers or not make any demands at all? Get in a taxi and ask for the nearest hospital? Should she call the police? Or should she simply back away as she had backed away from the theater, away from this gross violation of nature, this crime against the laws of physics, and forget that she ever saw such a thing in all her life?

The fact that the answer was not clear and primal spoke to all that had been left unfinished between them.

He abandoned the shadow and slipped inside the museum. She said nothing. She followed him, through the entrance and into an atrium, where he stopped by a large boat encased in glass. Nearby a guard in a dark green uniform stood tall. She could feel him watching, though of course there was no way for him to understand the sheer impossibility of what he was observing, that he was witness to a nightmare or a miracle, and the gap between her inner reality and the world around her felt so enormous she feared she was going to be swallowed up.

Her husband stared at the boat with great attention and longing. She watched the fluttering eyelashes, the pulsing jawline, the slope of his cheekbones. His bottom lip twitched in a way that would have been imperceptible to anyone but his wife.

She was afraid that if she spoke, he would disappear.

Where could they even begin?

Do you still find meaning in sunrises?

When did you start finding meaning in boats?

Are we even really here?

Richard, she said, because that was his name, Richard, the same name that had belonged to his grandfather. He had never gone by a nickname. He hated it when people made the mistake of calling him Dick or Richie or Rich.

With her pinkie she brushed the linen edge of his coat sleeve.

Richard, she said again.

He went up a winding marble staircase. She trailed behind,

the heels of her sandals clacking. They circled the first of five floors, past a life-size display of two revolutionaries slinking through the woods. The wax figures were clothed in fatigues. Clare had trouble finding their mouths. The museum curled around a courtyard, where a brass band was settling into folding chairs, tuning their gleaming instruments. When she glimpsed Richard again he was on the other side of this courtyard, one floor higher than she, a blotch of white hovering in the embrace of a window and then darting along.

She tracked him to the top floor, to a ballroom filled with tourists unfurling maps and photographing the hulking crystal chandeliers, the gilded frescoes of angels. Her husband broke into a trot. A couple with Australian accents stepped into the path between them, hands laced, a barrier of flesh and breath. Clare jumped. Shoved her way forward. Launched his name into the crowd. Outside the band had sprung into song. She left the ballroom in time to see her husband racing down the marble stairs. She chased him into the courtyard, past the musicians exhaling into gold horns, and out the back exit, the tails of his jacket flapping.

From the steps, Clare watched her husband hop onto a motorbike and veer into the traffic on Avenida Bélgica, zooming past a small square and lumbering tour buses and children playing soccer on the sidewalk, into the bright heat of the day. In the square, a woman reading on a bench looked up from her book, momentarily startled by the story unfolding before her. Clare had never before seen her husband operate a motorbike, but he navigated it like he had been riding one all his life, like he had been riding one in Havana all his life, like he had not been struck by a car and killed in the United States of America some five weeks ago.

In her former life, Clare was a sales rep for Thyssen-Krupp. Her area was elevator technologies and her territory was the Midwest. She liked the job because it involved an endless amount of travel to seemingly anonymous places. She had been to Nebraska forty-seven times. What was there to see in Nebraska? A surprising amount, really. She knew where to get the best steak in Omaha; when she cut into it, blood pooled on the white plate. She had seen dawn turn the plains as lustrous and vast as an ocean. Once, late at night, she parked her rental car on the side of the road and walked into a cornfield. She stood on a dirt path, surrounded by dark stalks, and imagined a harrowing chase through the corn that culminated in her murder at the hands of a masked killer with a knife. In the night sky, she spotted the red flash of planes through gossamer clouds, and if she listened very carefully, more carefully than she had listened to anything in months or maybe even in years, she was able to make out the dull roar of their passing.

She got back into her rental car and drove away and wondered if this was what people meant when they talked about
mindfulness.

Early in her career she learned that one of the most important rules of travel was this: the answer to nearly everything
could be found in the signs. This way to baggage claim. This
way to the ticket counter. This way to Cleveland. This way to
Omaha. This way to the hotel bar. Travel was one of the few
arenas in life where clear and correct direction was so readily
at hand.

Lately she had been tasked with selling a new kind of cable
to fine hotels and high-rise office buildings and factories. This
cable was made of carbon fiber and allowed elevators to travel
twice as fast as they could with steel.

They lived in New Scotland, a town on the outskirts of
Albany. In their condominium, she kept a small rolling suitcase in the bedroom closet, stocked with miniature toiletries,
exercise clothes, an inflatable neck pillow, and the book she
brought with her on every flight but could never seem to finish:
The Two Faces of January, by Patricia Highsmith. It wasn't an
especially long novel, but on planes she could only read a few
paragraphs before the words filled her with a crippling and
inexplicable dread, driving the book back down into the depths
of her shoulder bag. It was not so much the story that unsettled her, but the hidden things she sensed quivering under the
surface. Subtext, she supposed this was called, and she did not
care for it. Every time she saw her suitcase in the bedroom
closet, tucked behind a mesh laundry bin, she imagined it was
waiting for her second, secret self.

She traveled so frequently it was not uncommon for her to
wake in the middle of the night and think for a moment,
Where am I? She did not find this disconcerting, even when it

happened in her own bed, but once she made the mistake of mentioning those midnight thoughts to her husband and he looked at her like she was terminally ill.

The travel had long been a point of contention between them. Why bother being married if you're always leaving? A reasonable question, and she couldn't say that she had an answer, beyond the demands of her work. She wanted to be married and she wanted to leave; the two did not seem mutually exclusive. She had this second, secret self that she didn't know how to share with anyone, and when alone, that self came out into the open.

In the months before his death, her husband's own secret self started coming out into the open too; she could only assume this other self had been waiting inside him all along. The year of the great change: he was the same and he was different. The way he looked when asleep changed. His face used to be smooth and expressionless, almost masklike, but then one night she found him sleeping with lips parted into a wide, unsettling smile. He switched coffee mugs, trading out *The Exorcist* for the ghoulish face of Michael Myers. He was newly skittish around dogs, he stopped adding salt to his food, he stopped eating bananas, his pace on the sidewalk changed. He used to be a brisk, impatient walker, and then one day he began moving so slowly and contemplatively it was as though every tree branch was a source of wonder. Clare struggled to imagine what, forty years into a life, would cause a person to suddenly change the way they walked. There were alien, interminable silences when she called from the road, and when she was home he took long, solitary strolls in the evening hours, a symptom that would eventually lead to his demise.

Another symptom: he started demanding to know what she did on the road, how she accounted for all those hours alone, no matter how many times she told him the simple truth: in a hotel room her favorite thing in all the world was to switch off every light and everything that made a sound—TV, phone, air conditioner, faucets—and sit naked on the polyester comforter and count the breaths as they left her body.

Naked! her husband would shout, as though she had provided him with damning evidence. He had been an angry person for as long as she had known him, but it was a secretive anger; most people found him loose and lighthearted. "Easygoing"—that was the word people used, and in time she became suspicious of anyone who could be described in such terms. What was so easy about going?

Naked and *alone*, she would say back. Naked and alone.

As a married couple, they'd had perfect years and they'd had shit years, but she had never in her life experienced a year that so thoroughly dismantled her with confusion.

On her next trip, she thought about what he would see if he ever were to trail her on the road. A woman marking up sales reports with a pink highlighter. A woman watching workout infomercials with the volume on mute. A woman eating roomservice quesadillas in the bathtub, instead of reading that novel she claimed to be nearly finished with. A woman doing a little exercise routine—squats and sit-ups, bicep curls with bottled waters—completed with the hope that he would notice the smooth lines when he put his hands on her body. A woman breathing naked on the toilet seat. A woman breathing naked in an armchair. A woman breathing naked before the bathroom mirror, in the kind of lighting that could make a person reconsider every choice they had ever made in life. A woman breathing naked in the dark.

Torture the women, Hitchcock was reported to have said when a young director asked him for advice.

Before Richard submitted his papers for publication, he asked her to read them aloud. That was how she became familiar with his theories. They would sit together at the kitchen table, an amber finger of whiskey in mismatched juice glasses, and he would take notes while she read. She learned about Final Girls, those lone female survivors, and Terrible Places. The wilderness hut of Jason Voorhees, where he stored the mummified head of his mother. The subterranean slaughterhouse in *The Texas Chainsaw Massacre*. In the Terrible Place, the most hideous part of the nightmare unfolded. In the Terrible Place, the killer and the Final Girl were forced into their ultimate confrontation.

The papers were very long, and sometimes it would take hours for her to finish. She tried to concentrate on every word, feel the shape of each syllable in her mouth. Clare understood this tradition might have appeared strange or even sinister to outsiders, but she prized the chance to build together a sublanguage that ran, invisible and untranslatable, under the surface of the world.

At the time of his death, Richard was working on a book titled *The Nightmare Is Near: Urban Spaces in Horror*, an expansion of a paper presented at an important conference in Denmark. Her husband had grown up in small-town Arizona; for him, cities were a continuous well of fascination and dread. In rural horror, the terror lay in a literalized abyss, in the unseen nightmare that awaited deep in the desert or down that cave or out in the woods; you feared what you could not see. The urban gaze, however, was naturally multidimensional—the subway rumbling underneath the sidewalk; the gleaming peaks of skyscrapers; the neighbor's open window; the communal backyards—and so people tended to be confident in the accuracy of their sight. Yet who among them considered the networks of tunnels that ran under the subway or the basements that lurked under basements, the worlds stacked upon worlds stacked upon worlds. Who among them considered how these cities came into being in the first place. The layers of history accrued on the streets people walked to get to work or waltzed down to get to bars, the streets where murder victims bled and the drunk pissed and the homeless slept. From these unexamined quarters, her husband believed, horror sprung.

She had been invited to join him in Denmark but could not go because of an equally important sales conference in Minneapolis. When his attention was seized by the Festival of New Latin American Cinema and the inaugural screening of Yuniel Mata's film, she had received an invitation to Havana. A bridge was being offered, a bridge to the place where he now stood, and so what was she to do but say yes.

Clare never did have an affair on the road, but she did accumulate a lot of secrets about the odd things she had heard and seen. There were the dentures she discovered in the back pocket on a flight to Toledo, later removed by a flight attendant wearing blue rubber gloves. *People*, the flight attendant said, the imposter teeth suspended between her fingers. The midwestern hotels that could have belonged to a horror set, with their fluorescent hallways and lurching elevators and the eerie rattle of the ice machine in the middle of the night. The phone that rang on the hour in Wichita; when she picked up, no one was on the line. The receptionist in Cincinnati who told Clare that once a woman fell into such a deep sleep in this hotel, she never woke up. She didn't die, the receptionist clarified, slipping a room key into its little envelope, but went into some kind of coma and was taken out on a stretcher to a hospital somewhere and would likely be in this hospital for the rest of her life, on account of her having never woken up.

I don't think that story is good for business, Clare said as she took her room key.

The receptionist shrugged. The name tag pinned to her blouse read SAMANTHA. The more Clare looked at the tag, the more she got the uneasy feeling that SAMANTHA was not her real name.

Some people think it's the best story they ever heard, Samantha/Not Samantha said.

The very strangest thing happened in a hotel room in Omaha, in her beloved state of Nebraska. She opened the bedside drawer and next to the King James Bible lay a fingernail—so small that it could have only belonged to a pinkie, but fully intact and flawless in its shape. Her first impulse was to pick up the nail and swallow it, a thought so startling she slammed the drawer shut and turned on the TV and tried to watch an episode of *Law & Order* in which a man was suspected of killing both his first and second wives. Even though the cops found hard evidence, the killer ended up going free on a legal technicality and marrying for the third time.

She couldn't forget about the fingernail. She fell asleep with the drawer open, and all through the night she would wake up and turn on the bedside lamp and peer down at the nail. The light gave it a pearly translucence, made it look like a precious thing on display.

In hotels, she tried to be a respectful guest. Before leaving, she closed all the drawers and piled up the towels in the bathroom and recycled the paper coffee cups, but that morning she found she could not close the bedside drawer, could not seal the nail up in darkness again. As she wheeled her suitcase into the carpeted hall, she wondered what kind of person would abandon to a hotel room drawer such a perfect specimen of their existence.

She was three days back from a trip when her husband was struck by the car and killed. Her flight had landed in Albany at midnight, and when she returned to their condominium, she took a steaming hot shower and ate ice cubes in front of the TV. She fell asleep on the living room carpet, in a net of fluorescence, and when she woke in the morning he had left for school. She changed and drove to her office on Lake Street. She rode a sleek, fast elevator to the thirteenth floor. She ate a tuna fish sandwich at her desk. The afternoon brought a brief, driving rain.

There's something I want to tell you, her husband said that evening before he left for his walk. He had the lanky build of a track runner, though she had only ever seen him run to catch a train. Long fingers, high cheekbones, deep-set eyes. His hair was a honeyed blond, faded to corn silk at the temples. He was holding a yellow parka. His turtleneck was tucked in a little too tight. She noticed he was wearing the braided leather belt that had belonged to his brother. She had no idea where he went or what he thought about. Instead she respected his privacy, his desire for whatever solitary strangeness he was seeking, though later it would occur to her that maybe she had misjudged the situation and solitude wasn't what he wanted at all. Maybe he had been waiting for her to take an interest, inquire about his route, ask if he wanted company. In the months before his accident, she imagined he must have sensed himself plummeting toward some kind of end, must have felt the clawing panic that hits when you sense a part of your life is about to break off and drift away like an ice floe. *Who are you?* they seemed to always be whispering to each other, in this peculiar middle passage of their lives. *What are you becoming?* Neither of them had any idea he was on the edge of losing it all.

She said, Tell away, my love.

She had just finished lining up travel toiletries on the kitchen counter, to take stock of what needed replenishing. There was a tiny lipstick and a tiny soap and a tiny razor.

You came out of nowhere, asleep in front of the TV. He pointed at the living room carpet, as though she had just gotten up. For the last year, his expression had suggested he was thinking deeply about a problem he could not share. When I first came out and saw you there, it looked like you were unconscious. You scared me.

She uncapped the lipstick, stared down at the crimson nub. She could hear the lurking anger in his voice, hidden but no less deadly.

I *was* unconscious, she said. It's called being asleep.

Clare, he said. We need to talk.

She put her hands on her hips. She stared down at her toiletries. About what?

She told herself that she was not unwilling.

A door slammed. She looked up and found that he had left the room.

That night, he came back from his walk. The following night he did not. Two hours passed and she got a phone call from Memorial, and when she got there, he was in surgery, and when the surgeon came out to see her, he was dead. Hit and run.

Catastrophic internal bleeding. In the waiting room a TV was mounted on the wall and talk show hosts were playing golf on a miniature green. A man in a suit sank a white ball and the studio audience cheered. Scientists had discovered a planet believed to be larger than earth. A skull was found in a grocery in L.A., posed among the lettuces. Robots were being trained to read human minds. On the intercom, a doctor was being paged. Clare couldn't understand the surgeon. The bright white floor rumbled underneath her. She wanted to demand all these noises be stopped. He fought hard, the surgeon said, and for a moment she hallucinated him adding, *But he was no Final Girl.*

That one call from Memorial led to a succession of calls— to her husband's parents, in Arizona; to her own parents in Florida. Her mother had flourished in old age. She gardened and waterskied. She fostered American Bobtails and had taken to calling herself a "cat fancier." At the time of Richard's funeral, they had four Bobtails living with them in Jacksonville. Her father had no say in this cat fancying because the unalterable slide of dementia had transformed him into a furious, bewildered stranger. His own father had died from the same disease, with the same cruelly rapid onset; the end had been encoded inside him all along. There were no siblings to call. She was an only child and her husband's older brother had committed suicide by leaping from a bridge in California at age thirty-four. After her husband got that call, he wept through the night, in their bed, and she held him as tightly as she could. Looking back, she supposed that had been one miracle of their marriage—even if a person was on the brink of swallowing fingernails and the other was thinking deeply about a problem they could not share, there was still someone to hold you as you wept through the night.

———

At the funeral, they kept the casket closed, the polished dome heaped with lilies, and instead of sobbing she vomited before the service and after, over and over into the funeral home toilet, even though she hadn't eaten a proper meal in days. She kept seeing flashes from pregnancy possession horror, Mia Farrow eating raw chicken livers in *Rosemary's Baby*. She felt like someone had carved her heart out of her chest and then turned her loose to stumble through a dark forest on a frigid night. *I was here and now I'm going there. Where?* As a child, her father had read her *The Death of Ivan Ilyich* and those words bloomed in her mind like a miserable flower. Where was her husband now? Where was that *where*?

After the service, she wandered her own condo vaguely aware that her dress was crooked and her hair was tangled and her skin was pale and hot and gleaming, like she had been standing in front of a vegetable mister. There was a long run in her pantyhose and her breath stank. Her mother had cornered her father in the living room and was trying to feed him coffee cake, her pants feathered with cat hair. A month after her father's diagnosis, in the frozen middle of February, he had called Clare late one night. She'd answered in a hotel room in Omaha, standing in front of the TV in a T-shirt and socked feet. He told her that no one got through life without committing at least one unforgivable act and what he said next left her unable to speak in anything but sentence fragments for days; a new, broken language took hold. Her mother-in-law, now sonless, kept handing her plastic glasses of sweet white wine, which she kept abandoning on tables and counters. Her mother-in-law had insisted on a catered gathering, and now a waiter with a blond mustache was delivering her a butter cookie on a paper napkin with a slight bow, as though she was some kind of honored guest. DO YOU HAVE A BLOWTORCH? she wanted to ask her mother-in-law. DO YOU HAVE ANY KET-AMINE? Clare had a feeling her mother-in-law wished she would be a more graceful widow, that she would squeeze hands and kiss cheeks and thank people for their flowers and condolence cards and phone calls and prayers, even though the offer of prayer could be seen as adversarial if the offeree was not, in fact, religious. People who allegedly knew her kept resting hands on her shoulders and, in low, careful voices, asking about her plans. Would she like to take a walk or a yoga class or go see a movie? A movie! Would it be helpful if they brought over a casserole? For days she had been staying up all night watching Richard's extensive collection of horror movies, and by then every parking lot and alleyway and kitchen looked like an ideal place to be murdered.

WHAT IN THE FUCK ARE YOU TALKING ABOUT? seemed like the only rational response to these people who allegedly knew her.

Or: IN A HORROR MOVIE, YOU WOULD BE THE FIRST TO BE KILLED. YOU ARE THAT FUCKING DUMB.

I'm going, she kept hearing herself say. *I'm gone.*

The festival hotel was the first place Clare searched. She peered inside every conference room and into the face of every person she passed in the lobby and at the laminated badges beating softly against chests. She checked the men's bathrooms, feigning confusion when apprehended. She checked the theaters in Vedado designated for screenings: La Rampa, Yara, Charlie Chaplin. After Clare saw Richard, the invisible wall between her and *Revolución Zombi* had come crashing down, for the theater suddenly became the most probable place to find him in all of Havana.

At Cine Charlie Chaplin, she stood in a long line for the afternoon screening and took a seat in the very back. Whenever someone entered or exited, an attendant clicked on a flashlight, illuminating the path. Clare watched people move down the carpeted aisle, pause to select their seats. The film began and still no sign of her husband. She prepared herself to see a lot of blood.

Richard had been found by a Good Samaritan, on the part of Route 443 she knew as Delaware Avenue, just past Normans Kill and Graceland Cemetery, not far from where the road shot under the highway and became 9W. These details she had learned from the detectives assigned to the case: Detective Hall, a woman with a bleached pixie cut that did not suit her, and Detective Winter, a man who carried a coffee mug with the words DON'T ASK wrapped around the white belly. A crime had been committed, after all—perhaps intentional, perhaps accidental, but a crime nevertheless. The Good Samaritan was a high school chemistry teacher and a part-time EMT. He drove a pine-green station wagon. Unmarried. He had been the person to call 911, to wait with Richard for the ambulance. He said that on the side of the road her husband had been unconscious—*not with the world*, in his language. Richard did not respond to sound or touch or light. He did not speak. The Good Samaritan attended the funeral, and that was where he told Clare that he had held her husband's hand.

When the zombies first arrived, state TV claimed they were dissidents sent by the United States. The United States had interfered in their elections and in the revolution; now they were attempting an invasion. American occupation would not have been without precedent: twice the U.S. military had seized Cuba, once at the end of the Spanish-American War and again after Tomás Estrada Palma's administration collapsed in 1906, that second occupation summoning the first wave of American tourists, making the recent boom less a new phenomenon than a continuation in the giant loop of history.

There were two women in the film: a prostitute, whose death occurred within the first ten minutes and was treated like a joke, and the hero's estranged daughter, played by the possibly missing Agata Alonso. The daughter was visiting from Germany, where she lived with her mother. She was an elegant beauty, lithe and damp-eyed, and implied to still be a virgin. Clare herself had simple, pleasant looks—the kind of woman people might call pretty, never beautiful—and was certainly not a virgin but also not having sex all the time. In the average horror movie, she estimated her time of death would arrive approximately halfway through. *Revolución Zombi* had English subtitles, and Clare was relieved to be able to catch every word.

In Germany, the daughter was a blogger. In the early hours of the zombie plague, she spent her time complaining about the Wi-Fi and reading pirated foreign magazines. The government continued to blame U.S. dissidents until those officials were eaten up by zombies, an indomitable regime toppled in days. Then the hero devised a plan to video the zombie epidemic and smuggle the tape off the island, where it would be replicated and sold to the highest bidders. Their country had lied to them and had no plans to change. Why should they do anything to save it?

The hero's sidekick cracked a joke that made everyone laugh.

The sigh of the ocean washed through the theater.

The hero approached a stone tunnel blocked by an iron gate. He was in search of his mother, who had recently been made undead. A long shot of his face behind the rusted bars, the moment thick with suspension, and then he pushed the gate open, the hinges creaking, the darkness spreading before him like a body of water. The Terrible Place was near.

The screen flashed. Clare glanced down at her wrist and

became aware of an eel sliding around under her skin, just as Yuniel Mata had predicted. She leapt to her feet and rushed from the theater, the attendant's flashlight bright on her heels.

In the bathroom, she splashed water on her face. She pressed the underside of her wrist, as though she were taking her own pulse; the eel dove under the surface, fleeing her touch. In the mirror her reflection trembled. She pulled her eyelids apart. She poked her hot cheeks. She returned to the theater, but she did not take her seat. She watched the rest of the film standing in the shadows, her back to the door, a woman who could not decide if she was coming or going.

In order to survive long enough to film the zombie apocalypse and smuggle it off the island and make their fortune, the characters in *Revolución Zombi* had to keep battling the undead. Eventually the hero's sidekick was felled by zombies, not long after acquiring a gun that jammed before he could fire, which came as no surprise to Clare. Guns hardly ever worked in horror. They malfunctioned or went missing at critical times. Instead killers used knives and ice picks and axes and hammers and hypodermic needles and chain saws. Weapons that made them get close. At first, the daughter was not allowed to participate in all this killing, but after the hero confronted his undead mother in the tunnel, his tether to the old order was cut. Next thing Agata Alonso was carrying an ax and wearing combat boots and cut-off shorts, a knife sheath strapped to her thigh. She was sexier than she had been before but also less feminine, unlike the dead prostitute, last seen in lingerie and big hair.

Richard had once explained that many Final Girls had

androgynous names—Laurie, Ripley, Sidney—because to be less feminine than the other women, the ones who stupidly wandered into clammy basements and shadowed alleys and got gruesomely murdered, was crucial to their survival.

So you're saying to be feminine is to be weak and dumb? she asked.

To survive, it sounded like, the Final Girls had to be willing to transform into the men pursuing them.

Not exactly, he said. More like susceptible.

She had been reading one of his papers in the kitchen. Empty juice glasses. The clock ticking on the wall. The next day she was leaving for Racine, her small black rolling suitcase packed and standing watch in the front hall.

At the festival hotel, she located the information booth on the terrace and attempted to describe her husband to the woman sitting there.

He is forty years old. He is wearing a linen suit. He is an American.

She could not believe she was discussing him in the present tense.

She took out her cell phone and showed the woman a photo of Richard making marinara sauce in their kitchen. She could picture herself just outside the frame, standing by the stove and testing salt levels by licking pulverized tomatoes from the tip of the spoon. Did a person exist without photographic evidence? Not in this era.

She was aware that she was talking very fast.

The woman held an open umbrella, a small shelter from the sun. She had not seen anyone who fit his description.

Clare knew she had not been speaking clearly, the nuances

were getting lost, but to tell the story properly she would have to start in New Scotland, months before. If she were to keep pressing, if this woman were to summon someone from the hotel and if that person were to summon a police officer and if that officer were to ask when her husband had last been seen: nothing she knew in any language could sufficiently describe her situation.

She turned from the booth and walked straight into a congregating tour group, led by a guide in a pink visor. The guide raised a white flag and started for the lobby. In Clare's experience, most tours looked to either the past or the future; this one was invested in the past. In a circular marble hall, the guide drew the group's attention to an elevator rumored to be haunted. Clare followed them down a wide staircase, to an underground exhibit dedicated to the hotel's history. The movement of the group was snakelike, she the tip of the tail. The guide pointed to framed photos of movie stars smoking cigars on the terrace and foreign dignitaries and mobsters at the Havana Conference. Next a display on the Cuban Missile Crisis, including a map of the island that illustrated the former locations of the Soviet missiles with large red dots. The guide said that below the hotel lay a system of underground tunnels; they formed a stone circle beneath the outdoor gardens. During the crisis these tunnels had served as a bunker, with periscopes to keep watch on the U.S. Navy ships threatening invasion.

Glass display cases held newspaper headlines and photos of the tunnels. The group shuffled along, but Clare lingered on one photo in particular, a black-and-white image of a stone path leading to an iron gate. A tube of shadow behind the bars and then unending night. She leaned closer. She touched the glass. She severed herself from the group. She put her ear to the case, listened for the sigh of the ocean. She imagined peering through the rusted bars, like the hero had. A camera positioned in the shadows, the lens trained on her face. She wondered what the eye would see and what she would see in what the eye saw. She imagined the suspension transforming into a warm flood of inevitability as the gate swung open and she stepped into whatever new dislocation of reality lay ahead.

At the Third Hotel, she found a brochure for the National Zoo slipped under her door. She suspected it had come from Isa, who had made special mention of the zoo. When the front desk was quiet, Clare had noticed her reading an astronomy textbook, a trio of planets orbiting across the cover. Isa had pink highlights in her hair. She wore reading glasses with round frames, glasses that looked like they belonged to a much older woman, and T-shirts with sequined designs on the front; she had a beauty mark on her chin. In the mornings, when the front desk was hectic (the phone ringing, the front bell ringing, guests popping over from the breakfast room to inquire about more coffee or sliced papaya), she wedged her cell phone into the center of her bra for safekeeping. Her shoes were made for long hours on her feet, black clogs, the rubber heels worn thin as dimes. The hotel was technically a rambling casa, owned by extended family abroad and managed by Isa's cousins. Already Clare had observed a German college student delivering small gifts to the front desk: a guava candy one afternoon, a wilted pink carnation the next. Isa had eaten the candy and deposited the flower discreetly in the trash.

In her room, Clare stood by the phone on the bedside table. She pictured calling her mother in Jacksonville Beach, the Bobtails mewling in the background. She listened to the dial tone. She put the phone back down.

I did not see what I saw, she announced to the room.

In the bathroom, she dug cuticle scissors from her toiletries bag. The bedroom walls were a plain white, but the bathroom was printed with bright blue flowers and twisting green vines, the petals molting from the humidity. All day her hair had felt like an excess and undesirable weight. She began to nibble at the ends with the scissors, right where her hair dusted her collarbone. She nibbled up to the edge of making a terrible mess. She put the scissors away, shoving aside a desire to keep going until the white basin had been transformed into the pelt of an animal.

At Albany Memorial, Richard's possessions had been returned to her in a clear plastic bag. She had found, among his wristwatch and wallet and keys, a white cardboard box. It was the size of a small gift box, light in her hands. The edges were taped shut. She had brought it home and placed it on the kitchen table. Had he been on his way to see someone? Did the box indeed contain a gift? She sat, stood, circled the table. She felt unable to open it. She could not imagine what might be inside, and this inability to imagine felt damning to her somehow, a lethal failure of understanding. She had brought the box with her to Havana, nested in her backpack. During the flights she had unzipped her bag and peered down at the flat white top, the sealed edges. At the Third Hotel, she had placed it in the safe in her room. She liked the idea of the box living behind a locked door.

After Richard died, Clare had fantasies about figur-
ing out a way to live exclusively on airplanes. For
years, she had believed that if she just kept moving
she could elude the most painful parts of life, and now she had
come under the equally suspect belief that movement could
shield her from the most painful part of the most painful part.
On her last work trip, she'd vomited through the flight, in the
tiny airplane bathroom, even though she had never before been
airsick. She became one of the strange things other people
saw during their travels—the strangeness they talked about, or
didn't, when they returned home.

She spent around two hundred days on the road every
year, though she had not left the country unaccompanied since
college (with Richard: Glasgow; Mexico City; Lisbon; with
her parents, a budget cruise to Bermuda, which left her hoping
to never experience the grotesqueries of cruise travel again).
It was not until Havana, however, that she realized professional

travel and personal travel were sharply separated by a single fact: one realm contained directives, the other did not. She woke feeling like her brain had grown a layer of wool overnight. She would spend all day trying to cut the wool away and then the moment she fell asleep it came right back. Her hair thinned when she brushed it, matting the plastic teeth. A molar had gone loose in the back of her mouth. Her ability to rely on signage was breaking down. Beyond the borders of the old part of the city, where street names were painted on bright tiles, she had seen street signs written on rocks or on the sides of buildings or she had not been able to locate them at all.

The only directive she could find for herself here was movement, for while movement could lead her in the entirely wrong direction, she could not count on stillness to bring her any closer to the *where*.

She thought often of those pigeons in Plaza de San Francisco, circling and circling.

On her map, the city was shaped like the head of a dog. Every morning she started on the Malecón, near the Anti-Imperialist Plaza, where a statue of José Martí clutching Elián González overlooked the sparkling sea. The wall prevented her from getting lost, so she would trace that border between land and water all the way down into the old part of the city, with its scrubbed boulevards and elegant stone plazas and souvenir shops selling Che refrigerator magnets. At Plaza de la Catedral, a nativity scene had been arranged on the steps of a grand cathedral with twin bell towers, on a blond bed of straw. She had paid a small fee to enter the church, and learned that one bell had come from Spain, the other from Matanzas. If she was nearby when the bells sounded, she felt like she was being shaken. Plaza de Armas was bordered with stands displaying books for sale, the stands bordered by carriages resting in the shade, the rear hoofs of horses cocked. Each stand offered a variation on the same items: posters for the winter cinema and jazz festivals, novels, books about the revolution, some in laminated jackets, the plastic soft with dust. Persistent vendors tried to sell her on Hemingway.

If you leave a woman, though, you probably ought to shoot her, Hemingway had once written in a letter.

On Dragones, in the high heat of the afternoon, she slipped inside a hotel and, from the edge of a mezzanine bar with potted palms and fleur-de-lis tile, she watched a few minutes of CNN, in the blessed cool of the air-conditioning. On one side of the bar, a temperature-controlled mahogany chest held rows of cigars for sale. At a small table, a woman in a lunatic print ate a salad and sipped a cuba libre through a fluorescent pink straw.

Once she passed the white dome of the capitol and the baroque spires of the national theater, the buildings were pressed tight together and the window grates were being strangled by vines and the sidewalks and streets were trenched and pitted. Doorless entryways. Freestanding facades. Windows with head-size cavities. Through an open door she glimpsed a mammoth crumbling staircase, a decapitated statue rising from a banister, that led to a rooftop restaurant reported to be popular with tourists, ruin reborn as atmosphere. She looked up and saw men in rope harnesses scaling a building under construction. Close to the ocean a mist hung in the air. And then she was back in Vedado, trekking past the Ministry of Labor and Paradiso, the tourism bureau, and the lines outside the Coppelia ice-cream parlor, awaiting scoops of chocolate, pineapple, almond. Down Avenida de Los Presidentes, where she had spotted tourists posing before a statue of Abraham Lincoln. She walked this same avenida late one night and found it transformed, overtaken by young people with Mohawks and wallet chains, like a gathering of nineties anarchists.

She continued to notice jarring contrasts in architecture. A modern, glass-fronted boutique selling designer luggage across the street from housing overcome by crumble and mildew, bundled in treacherous-looking wiring. It was as though a second city were being constructed alongside the original, accessible to only a precious few.

Clare saw codes over doorways that she did not understand, street art signatures that she did not understand. To be foreign here meant to have access only to the uppermost layers of language, to what could be said aloud in public, and she understood that her very presence could turn a moment public, even if she was standing in someone's home.

She counted soaring gothic arches; neoclassical stone lions; bright art nouveau facades with ornamental moldings that made her think of Fabergé eggs; retro oceanside hotels; stark highrises. This collision of visuals meant that if someone were to ask after her impression of Havana, it seemed the most honest answer would be to admit there was no impression, not yet. A photographer, and she had seen many people taking photographs, could arrange this city to look however they wanted: nostalgic, luxurious, devastated, avant-garde.

Some forms of watching were designed to obliterate the subject.

She walked the same route for two days.

She visited the Colon Cemetery, a hundred-acre labyrinth of slim paths and marble mausoleums with spires like miniature churches. Statues of angels, stone wings flung open. She found the grave for Tomás Gutiérrez Alea, the great director. How shameful it now seemed for her husband to have been buried deep in the ground, in a simple coffin, no monument erected in his name—and even that simple burial had been shockingly expensive. She left the cemetery when her thoughts shifted to how easy it would be for a killer to hide behind one of those great stone graves, clutching an ice pick.

She saw films playing at the festival that were not *Revolución Zombi*. Films about teenage punks in Colombia and sheep ranchers in Argentina.

One film, she'd read, had been barred from the festival, a drama about the state's persecution of queer artists and intellectuals after the revolution—despite a script for this very same film having received an award from the festival two years earlier. The Cuban Institute of Cinematographic Art and Industry was established three months after the success of the revolution, a testament to the state's belief in the power of the screen, and the current director of the institute had called this film *a rewriting of history*—as though history was not being rewritten all the time.

At night, she tallied the streetlights that had long ago gone dark. She glimpsed a woman in a yellow spandex dress leaning into a car window, a leg bent at the knee as though she might lose her balance, fall inside. At first, she'd looked like a grown woman, but when she turned from the car and into the moonlight Clare saw that she was very young.

One evening, she sat alone at the festival hotel, the terrace bar atypically quiet because of an exclusive mid-festival party at an undisclosed locale—a ticket for this party had not been included in the information she'd received and it was not something she could buy. VIP, lady, she had been told. VIP. A famous American director had landed in Havana that morning, and she wondered if he was presently among these VIPs, perhaps in the company of the less famous American directors who'd come to mentor new Cuban talent, via labs sponsored by Sundance. The mention of the VIP party reminded Clare of the articles she'd read on the Havana Biennale, held that summer. Apparently there were glamorous parties in the Swiss and Norwegian embassies, and the biennale ushered in the first museum exchange between Cuba and the United States in decades—plus a new wave of collectors, thirsty for discovery.

On the terrace, a scattering of people sat in bamboo armchairs, studiously reading scripts. A woman clutching a cellophane-wrapped bouquet of red roses wandered around, looking for someone, it seemed. The sun had bled out into the Malecón and the water looked like velvet, like it would be soft to the touch. Already Havana was among the most beautiful places she'd ever seen the sun go down.

A man sat at the table next to her, in jeans and a T-shirt that read KEEP CALM AND SAIL ON. A gold band squeezed his ring finger. His hair was buzzed, exposing an egglike head. She couldn't remember the last time she'd seen a person so pink, with white ribbons of sunscreen collecting along his hairline.

Do you have the time? he asked, in English.

No one has the time. Clare knew a fake question when she heard it.

He wagged a finger at her like she was a naughty child.

A waiter arrived to collect drink orders, and then the man started going on about how this city would soon be ruined, would soon bear little resemblance to the place Hemingway had described in his books—wasn't she glad they'd come when they had? Her ear caught on that insidious *they*, the suggestion of alliance.

Clare was born in Georgia, in the barrier islands, where

her parents had managed a bed-and-breakfast. She remembered the way guest after guest shrank her home to fit their version—paradise, tourist trap—uninterested in local consultation. In her opinion, this was the lot of islands. In Havana, the signals were manifold and often contradictory, making it easy for a person to find support for whatever narrative they had decided to seek.

Soon there'll be Internet, the man continued. Our phones will work. He pulled a black smartphone from his pocket and wagged it at her. The shackles will be back on, like they are everywhere else. Where's the romance in that?

The past is a product, Clare said. So is romance.

In her world, for example, there had recently been a hunger for elevators with a vintage look.

Or maybe the real product was nostalgia—even if people tended to be nostalgic for periods of time about which they knew little. It was, in fact, this not-knowing that made such a candied nostalgia possible. When Clare was ten, her parents relocated to Jacksonville Beach, to manage an inn called the Seahorse (even as a child she'd understood this move to Florida was not a promotion). The inn had wallpaper in the rooms that bore a striking resemblance to the cobalt flowers and green vines in the bathroom of the Third Hotel, and here they had all participated in putting nostalgia up for sale. Be transported back to Old Florida, with natural beaches and fish camps; a little farther south, the oldest masonry fort in America, no mention of its bloody history. Visitors longed for not a dislocation of reality but an insulation from reality—yet these layers of insulation were supposed to be invisible, imperceptible. People did not like to be too sharply reminded of their status as tourists. For years, she was charged with combing the Seahorse's TripAdvisor reviews for problems; the word she counted the most frequently in the positive reviews was "authentic."

Also: comfortable, accommodating, spotless, secure, safe.

If reviewers praised the service at reception as "welcoming," they had interacted with Clare's mother, who used her goodwill up on strangers. Her father hoarded his and then sent benevolence out like an unexpected flare.

Our phones make sure we know too much and too little all at the same time, the man went on.

You can try getting Wi-Fi on the Malecón. Clare pointed at the water ahead.

Earlier she had seen people sitting on the seawall with their phones. She carried a small pair of binoculars in her backpack and considered handing them to this man, so he could look for himself. All he had to do was get an ETECSA card, assuming the kiosks hadn't run out for the day, and head to the seawall or a Wi-Fi park. Her cell carrier only offered stupendously expensive pay-as-you-go service on the island, so she was just using her phone for the offline map she'd downloaded (and found to be largely inaccurate) and for photos; at night she would scroll through images of Richard, shrinking and enlarging, searching for clues. She had not checked her e-mail or his since arriving. In order to access Richard's e-mail, she'd had to submit a copy of his death certificate to Decedent Accounts, and it had been deeply painful for her, to write to Decedent Accounts. To be unable to guess her own husband's password, even after trying all the birthdays and addresses and film titles and family names and inside jokes. To learn the password was a sequence of numbers that held no meaning for her at all.

On the terrace, the man waved her off. I don't want to know. If I know, I'll have to contact my wife.

And why don't you want to contact your wife? Now, Clare thought, they were getting somewhere.

He and his wife had arrived in Havana together and had been scheduled to continue on with a tour to Viñales, but they had fought and she had gotten on the bus without him.

What was the fight about?

To answer that question I'd have to start with the day we met, he said. We'd be out here all night. He added that travel turned his wife into a different person and she loved to travel, loved getting to be that other person, but he dreaded meeting this unpleasant twin and would be content to never go anywhere again.

Their drinks arrived. He tipped his glass toward Clare. She raised her glass in return, a mistake because next he asked if he could treat her to a meal, his tone entreating and paternalistic, a two-front attack: first, elicit pity for his sad situation; second, instill doubts about her ability to navigate the coming night. Wouldn't it be nice if her dinner was simply handled? Had he not raised the subject of Hemingway, she might have taken him up on his offer, and the offer she sensed would follow, for the way crashing against his pink body would rip thoughts from her head like weeds, would make her feel sick in an entirely different way.

The sky was dark. Through the trees she glimpsed silver lights on the water. They looked like the lights from a cruise ship. A rooster screamed somewhere next door. An elderly couple wearing white surgical masks sat at a table nearby, freshly emerged from another world.

Good luck with your wife, Clare said, but he was already scanning the other tables, assessing his options.

She tucked money under her glass and hurried down the terrace.

By the water she saw that the lights had been an illusion: the cruise ship was not a cruise ship at all. A white wedding tent had been erected on the far edge of the terrace, strung up with silver lights. The bride and groom stood at the front, facing each other. The bride wore a knee-length white dress with a lace hem; huge taffeta sleeves stood up on her shoulders like a pair of meringues. The groom wore a jacket and shirt, no tie. She could not tell who was conducting the ceremony; maybe that person had yet to arrive on the scene. She wondered if this couple knew they were getting married above tunnels used in the Cuban Missile Crisis and in *Revolución Zombi*. All the guests were standing, and she found the attire peculiar. Ball gowns and black tie alongside untucked button-downs and jeans. There was a story here, but not one she could access. Perhaps the ceremony had been assembled in a hurry.

My husband.

In her correspondences with Decedent Accounts and the bank and the car insurance company, she did not say "Richard has died" but "my husband has died." They did not care about who he had been but rather their relationship to his death and the role she now expected them to play in it. In the moments when she had said "Richard" aloud it had felt like a mistake, like trying to call a number that had been disconnected. "My husband" reminded her that he was no longer a person moving through the world, but a void, a hole dug deep in the ground, a tear in the atmosphere.

At the Third Hotel, Clare got into bed and slid into a state of unconsciousness that did not quite feel like sleep, and when she woke the sky was dumping rain. *Where am I?* She had not experienced that thought since arriving, as though the city remained inescapable even when bundled in the twilight of unawakeness. She turned onto her side and thought about driving with Richard out to Grafton Lakes, as they sometimes did. They would walk the frozen ground and look out at the lake, the ice silver and crackling. They would watch the sun go pale. They thought this place was most beautiful in winter, and given how rarely they saw another person at Grafton Lakes, they understood this love of winter beauty was a sentiment few people shared. On the way home they would stop at a gas station for coffee and share a cup in the car. They stopped at signs for garage sales too—they found an oil painting of a roaring sea in Sycaway, a watercolor of a train station in Troy. Once she emerged from the depths of a cavernous garage, a glazed vase tucked under her arm, and could not find her husband on the sidewalk or browsing the tables. It turned out he had gone to the corner store at the end of the block for a snack, and in the time before he returned, she was seized by the terrifying thought that she had dreamed their entire marriage. Sometimes, if Clare was just back from a trip, she would fall asleep in the passenger seat, slumped against her husband, and she would feel very warm. She remembered Richard waking her in their driveway, his hands in her hair, his breath on her neck, his voice saying *Clare*. She felt a mist on her skin. Was someone spraying her? No, it was coming from the balcony, a blade of rain-soaked night visible through the open door.

The next afternoon, Clare's walking route led her to Parque John Lennon. On the edge of the park, a man in an AC/DC shirt sold disposable razors to passersby. She stood at the foot of a bronze statue of John Lennon sitting on a bench, translating a commemorative plaque in the shade of royal poincianas. A man in slacks and a checkered shirt appeared and sat next to the statue. He was carrying a black case, the kind that might hold a musical instrument, a clarinet or a flute. Did she want to see John Lennon's glasses? He formed two circles with his fingers and pressed them to his eyes, lashes fluttering as he spoke. She wondered how John Lennon came to have a monument in Havana. Was it the sole purpose of this man to oversee the glasses? She told him yes, she would like to see these glasses very much.

He opened the case, lifted out a pair of bronze glasses from the black velvet interior, and slipped them onto John Lennon's face. The longer Clare stood before him, the more she felt certain she had seen this man somewhere before, and then it came to her: he had been an extra in *Revolución Zombi*. He had tried to attack Agata Alonso in a garden, and she had dispatched him with a shovel.

The man asked if she wanted to take a photo, and while Clare was contemplating the possibility of a photo, she noticed a woman passing on the sidewalk. She was walking quickly in wedge sandals, hands deep in the pockets of loose black pants, face shielded by cat-eye sunglasses. She wore a sleeveless navy tank, and it was her shoulders that caught Clare's attention: slim and graceful, shaped with the precision of sculpture. She had seen those precise shoulders somewhere before too. She had seen them on a movie screen in Cine Charlie Chaplin.

The eel whispered: *movement*.

Clare could ask if Agata Alonso had chosen to vanish herself from the festival or if she was in some kind of trouble; on this front, progress could be made. She could apologize for fleeing the theater in the middle of the movie, for drawing the viewer's attention away from her image on the screen. She could compliment her performance as the virginal daughter; she could say that she did not blame her character at all for living with her mother in Germany. Her father, frankly, seemed to be a bit of an asshole.

She excused herself from the man and John Lennon's glasses.

She sprinted across the park and fell behind Agata Alonso on the sidewalk. Her hair was not the copper bob that Clare had seen on-screen and in the press photos. Instead she wore a long wig, the frosted blond ends striking her shoulder blades.

On the corner of Avenida Paseo, not far from the sea, the actress slipped inside a pistachio-green house with cream moldings and an enclosed front garden that reminded Clare of a giant birdcage. Behind the bars pink bougainvillea slumped across a metal trellis and a fat black cat with a gold bell sunned itself on a stone bench. From the street, she tried to get a look through the windows, but the blinds were closed tight. The cat rolled onto its back, batted a paw at a column of dust. A powerful wind tore down the avenida. She smelled overripe fruit and salt. Thanks to the heavy bamboo blinds, the windows were impenetrable; she could not see so much as a silhouette or a shadow.

Another evening at the festival hotel, another reception in the lobby. Without even sitting down, let alone falling asleep, Clare dropped a layer below consciousness, into a dream in which she was descending an unending staircase; every time it seemed that she was getting close to the bottom, a dozen more marble steps unfurled at her feet. When she was no longer dreaming, she was halfway down the mezzanine stairs, an empty glass in her hand. She spotted Davi, the critic she'd sat next to on the plane. He was standing by the forest mural and talking to Arlo—who, she imagined, would prefer to not see her anywhere near the mural.

Earlier, in the drink line, Arlo had been in front of her. From eavesdropping, she'd gleaned he was from Havana but had been away. He'd been recently approved for a job with the ICAIC, he told one person, where his uncle enjoyed a well-placed position. After that person left the line and he was greeted by someone else, he claimed to have returned because his twin sister had decided to commit suicide at the age of thirty-three, like her idol Hart Crane.

There are tunnels under our feet, Clare told the bartender when it was her turn, and got no reply.

When Davi saw Clare coming, he raised his glass in greeting. His hair was damp and combed back. His shirt was cuffed at the wrists, showing off a handsome watch. Her gaze flitted over the gold-tinged treetops of the forest mural. Her pulse quickened, her tongue dampened and swelled. She felt driven to do things with her body that she did not understand.

You *know* the mural kisser? Arlo rattled the ice in his glass. He had a powerful nose, delicate eyelashes. He and Davi had been speaking in Spanish, though the moment she appeared Arlo had switched into fluid English—a rebuke, she assumed, of her language skills.

Seatmates. Davi smiled and shrugged, as though sitting next to a person on a plane obligated you to enter into a pact of continued companionship.

In the lobby, she was reminded of Davi's perfect eyebrows, which she suddenly wanted to touch. He deposited his glass on a side table and said they were leaving for an art opening. Did she want to come? It would be a prodigious good time. His smile was different from the pitying one he offered her on the plane. Now it was curious, playful, solicitous. Women traveling alone were often the subjects of curiosity; this she had learned during all those trips to Nebraska.

Any chance Yuniel Mata might be there? she asked.

After the press event, she had only seen the director once more. She had glimpsed him through her binoculars, cloaked in black sunglasses and slipping into a yellow cab.

Anything is possible, Davi said.

Arlo pantomimed slitting his wrists with his festival badge.

We used to work together, Davi said. In Rio.

Davi, in addition to being a critic, also produced documentaries. In Rio, he and Arlo had worked together on a doc about a famous Brazilian photographer. Through a network of connections and invitations that seemed vague to Clare, Arlo, who had attended film school in Havana, had been coming and going from the city for some time—a year in Rio, six months in Buenos Aires, ten in Barcelona.

Now I'm an experiment, he said. An experiment in being a person who stays.

Experiment with being a person who *stays in Rio*, Davi said, nudging him in the ribs. That is your path to happiness.

It was clear to her that this conversation about Arlo's whereabouts had been ongoing between the two of them; for a moment she was being permitted to interlope.

We'll see, Arlo said. We'll see if I'm ready to meet that person.

He turned to Clare and told her that he'd come home to make a documentary on light fixtures.

All I want on the screen, Arlo said, is the present tense. Anything is possible in the present tense. Failure and love and stillness and change.

He's an artist, Davi said. Artists are mercenaries.

At that line, the men laughed and laughed.

In the taxi, Arlo took the front, she and Davi tumbled into the back. They raced along the Malecón, the ocean following like a shadow. She could hear water thrashing against the seawall and remembered reading that twice the city was founded in the middle of a swamp; twice it was moved from its original site before settling on the island's northern coast. She held her purse in her lap and through the cloth she felt the envelope of cash she carried, as her American credit cards were worthless here. Soon the envelope would be empty, but not yet.

In the passenger seat, Arlo was telling the driver a story about his great-uncle, who had been an economist and who traveled periodically to Paris, where he always ended up lovesick and jumping off bridges. Six different bridges through the years, according to the family story, and still he lived. No one was luckier than this great-uncle. Finally, in Havana, he met a woman and they married. At last, true love! Not long after the wedding, he fell ill with cancer and died. When Arlo got to the end, the driver, to Clare's surprise, seemed to find the story quite amusing.

The window was cracked open, and all of a sudden she was pressing her face into the gap like an animal sniffing the air, the oceanic rot, and willing the driver to go faster, faster. She wanted a speed great enough to hurtle them into a space beyond the limits of time, a space in which she would be free of past and future, of memory and feeling, though of course she realized such a state did exist and it was called Being Dead.

The taxi clunked over a pothole, knocking her back into the conversation.

Arlo and Davi were discussing a producer who'd worked on *Revolución Zombi* and was loathed by the crew. Yuniel Mata's film had not relied exclusively on the ICAIC. Funding had also been secured through a collaboration among three production companies: one Spanish, one Cuban, one Italian. In the eighties, Clare remembered, there had been a rage for uncut versions of grisly Italian horror films. Some were styled as pseudodocumentaries; in one particularly objectionable instance, the footage looked so real that the director was rumored to have killed his own actors on set.

The producer from the Italian company had been the problem, according to Arlo and Davi. Apparently he had forced Agata Alonso to drink cow's blood to get into character—even after she vomited and cried.

The art opening was in a renovated olive oil factory with a brick smokestack and tall windows that glowered over the Almendares River. The line to get in coiled around the block. Once inside, they picked up white squares of paper from a counter, used by the bartenders to record drink orders.

Don't lose it, Davi said, holding up his square. Or it'll cost you.

If you lost your card, you had to pay thirty pesos. Apparently tourists lost their cards all the time here and then argued the consequences.

She followed her new companions through a labyrinth of halls and rooms. A doorway led to a staircase; a staircase led to a room and then tapered into a hall; a hall opened into a room adjacent to the one they had just crossed, with a window that allowed her to glimpse the people standing where she had stood moments before, the entire layout designed to encourage the viewer to cast an eye back on their own path or to forget the notion of a path at all. Everywhere there were paintings and photographs and mobiles and screens and the island of Cuba made entirely of brass keys and a tiny alcove boutique selling handmade jewelry and shoes. Worlds stacked upon worlds. A vast room with rows of chairs, the backs to a fluorescent-lit bar, connected the two halves of the space. They passed through this room twice, and each time something different was happening: a brass quintet; a skateboarding documentary playing on a giant screen. According to Davi, the factory had been open only for a year and it was not state run or privately owned—the government owned the land, while the art galleries and the bars were classified as private businesses. It was a new kind of experiment, an in-between space, a delicate, delicate dance.

They got beers and mojitos from a bar and then climbed a flight of stairs to the exhibit. Ten large black-and-white photographs hung on white walls, each an image of other people taking pictures. In one, a woman kneeled on a split sidewalk, a digital camera pressed to her face like a mask. In another, two young women trained cameras on the ground; they appeared to be photographing a pothole. In another, a couple held phones in front of their bodies, unclear if they were photographing whatever lay ahead or taking a selfie. In fact, there were two layers of anonymity: the subjects of the subjects were excluded, left to the viewer's imagination, and also the subjects did not appear to be aware they were just that. One exception was a middle-aged woman holding a long-snouted Canon, captured at the exact moment she registered the weight of another camera's eye, her face warped by the beginning of a glare. Her upper lip had curled just enough for Clare to see that she wore adult braces.

While cleaning out Richard's home office, Clare had come across a Super 8 camera in the bottom of a cabinet drawer, covered in loose papers. The camera was black and gun-shaped, a birthday gift she had not seen him use in years.

Screens were vehicles for the subjective, he had once written. No eye was objective and thus no lens could be either. In turn, the viewer's response to the images became the third subjective eye, an invisible revelatory force. Screens and images revealed the viewer as much as they revealed *to* the viewer. Who in this gallery was being struck still by currents of pleasure or guilt or rage. Who was looking at the subject with the long-snouted Canon and thinking she resembled their mother. Who thought this and felt bowed with love. Who felt murder in their heart. Who gazed at the pair of young women and wished they could see through their tops.

She'd lost track of Arlo and Davi. She wandered down two flights of concrete stairs, through a hall and a set of swinging doors and into a dance party, the walls pulsing with reggaeton. On the ceiling a scattering of fluorescent stars. She forgot about Yuniel Mata and thought instead that this might not be a bad place to keep an eye out for Agata Alonso; if the actress was lying low, it would be easy to hide in these shadowed crowds. A man delicately pinched the back of her elbow and then disappeared. She looked at the shimmering heads of the men around her, some in pairs or buoyant groups, some standing alone, holding drinks close to their bodies. *Richard*, she thought for a moment, the shadow of the touch still hot on her elbow, and then, *No, no, no.* She got another drink and sucked the straw until the plastic was ragged, her throat numb. Strobe lights cut around, and after they illuminated a young couple tangled against a wall, she crouched on the floor, lungs burning for air.

Out and up through the vast room, where footage from a Nirvana concert had taken over the screen, and onto a concrete landing. People were clustered in the corners, washed in blue light, blowing smoke into the green fronds of plants. Along one wall, a trio of small, square windows looked into a private restaurant available only to special guests, according to a sign, a pocket of exclusivity in the otherwise democratic-seeming world of the art factory. A bronze statue stood in the center of the landing—a tall figure in a cape, a woman, a wraith. Enormous black tires surrounded the statue and were being used as benches.

In front of the statue, the eel shot down her spine. The bronze figure had no face.

Liesel! a voice exclaimed from behind. Damp hands clamped

down on her shoulders. The voice had pronounced the name like a long sigh. *Lee-zeel.*

Clare turned to face a British woman with floppy blond curls and a grotesque sunburn. She was wearing a linen scoop-neck dress, sleeveless, the skin on her chest and shoulders crimson and molting. The slope of her nose looked like it had been boiled.

Liesel, the woman said again. Why didn't you tell me you'd be here?

She raked a hand through her curls. Her jaw flexed. She was perturbed, but trying to not show it. The kind of person, Clare imagined, who ground her teeth in her sleep.

So, she said. Are you here with another group?

Clare tilted her head. Another group?

Through yet another window, on the opposite side of the landing, she glimpsed the room below, the dance floor undulating with bodies. She had been one of those bodies—right until she felt the eel slide up her sternum and snug itself around her throat.

If a person starts out a group traveler, they usually stay a group traveler, the British woman said. She carried a red tote with a decal that read KING'S TRAVEL CO.

It's hard to change, she continued, once you've gotten used to having literally everything handled for you.

Well, there is no other group, Clare said. I'm here alone.

She was starting to understand: groups were the British woman's business, and she was hurt by the prospect of Liesel having defected to a different provider.

The British woman told Clare that people said all kinds of things at the end of the tour, when they were feeling sentimental. How they had had the time of their lives and it was all because of her.

Imagine! she said. Me giving someone the time of their lives.

She drew a cigarette from the front pocket of her dress and lit it.

Good for you for making the hop, she went on. The first time I came here I hitchhiked all around, not a guide for miles. Tomorrow I'll meet a group at José Martí and take them hither and yon. But why am I telling you all this, Liesel? I'm sure you remember.

Clare was curious about this Liesel. Possibly of German ancestry. Possibly American, as the British woman had not commented on her accent. Possibly a current resident of the U.K. She imagined Liesel living in a town in Wales, Cardiff, or Swansea. She imagined her driving a diminutive car through roundabouts. She imagined her drinking a beer on the beach at sunset, her hair thick with sea. Did she work as a librarian or at a bank? Was she a retired assassin? Did she have a cat?

On the landing, Clare became aware of a man beside her. She did not acknowledge him right away because she was unsure of what Liesel would say, how she would handle such a sticky situation.

Liesel? The British woman tapped her sandaled toe against Clare's shin. Is this a friend of yours?

This is Arlo, Clare said, grasping his elbow. He's an artist, which means he's also a mercenary. She tried to smile and found that the muscles in her face had been immobilized.

Arlo wrested his arm from Clare, with a sharpness that made the eel turn summersaults in her gut, but he did not disrupt the story. The British woman introduced herself as Bryony.

I was just about to ask after Liesel's family, Bryony said next. A pity I only got to see them in photos.

The knowledge of a family disrupted Clare's previous image of Liesel. Now there was a station wagon passing through the roundabouts, small paper rafts filled with chips at the beach.

Yet her family had not accompanied her to Havana, given that Bryony knew them only through photos. Clare wanted to turn from the conversation, to wonder over their absence, but Arlo and Bryony were both leaning toward her, expectant. Arlo, who seemed amused by the trap he'd found her stuck in, added that he too was curious to know about her family, if they were well.

Something she and her husband had in common but rarely discussed was the absence of a desire for children, to fill their home with people besides themselves. It was a silent agreement, felt rather than spoken, and in her experience the soundest agreements were the ones that did not require the reassurances of language. Therefore this line of questioning was the inverse of what she usually fielded, since a childless married woman in her thirties was so often regarded, by men and women alike, as a puzzle or a pity. *What's the story here?* people would ask, inquests designed to make women like her suspect there was something malformed inside, blinding them to the hideous reality of their choice.

She turned her wedding ring on her finger. She imagined the beach in Wales, the cardboard raft of chips, the small hands grabbing at the golden shells. Liesel crawling inside the now-empty cardboard raft and paddling out to sea.

Everyone is very well, she said, the eel skittering across her heart.

In the vast room, a Jimmy Stewart film had taken over the screen. The light on the landing shifted, and Bryony's sunburn turned an even more alarming shade of red, like she had been exposed to radiation and gone phosphorescent.

So how do you two know each other? Bryony pointed her cigarette at Clare and then at Arlo.

I've come home to make a documentary about suicides in Havana, Arlo said. Liesel here is part of my crew.

Ah! So you're here for work. Bryony stamped out her cigarette, the mystery of why Liesel had not returned to Cuba with a tour group at long last solved.

But I don't recall you working in film, she added.

Well, Clare said, I do.

Havana has a remarkable history of suicides, Arlo continued. We've lost a number of mayors, for example. Take Supervielle, ruined by his failed promise to build an aqueduct. A personal favorite is Chibás, the politician who committed suicide during his own radio program, though sadly he lost track of time and ended up firing the fatal shot during a commercial break. Even the cats commit suicide here. Watch and you'll see them leaping from balconies. The contagion is now threatening my own sister, who is planning to commit suicide at the age of thirty-three, like Hart Crane. In the meantime, she works as a mammal trainer at the National Aquarium and spends her free time skateboarding in a drained swimming pool, life choices I do not pretend to understand.

Bryony frowned. Below, the pulse of the music intensified.

Clare knew nothing of skateboarding except one bad joke. What did the skater say who fell and broke her elbow? That wasn't very *humerous*.

Hart Crane is her favorite poet, Arlo said, with a shrug. Personally I prefer one of my countrymen, Nicolás Guillén.

As you can see, this is a very personal project, said Clare.

I could go on, Arlo said.

Please don't, said Bryony, wrinkling her nose.

Do you even have a sister? she would have asked Arlo had they been alone.

Hart Crane didn't leave a suicide note, Arlo continued. He spoke his last words before jumping from a ship. Goodbye, everybody!

Straight to the point, Clare said. No time for bullshit.

This is simply not the Liesel I remember, Bryony said. She took a step closer to Clare, her blue eyes narrowing. Have you done something different with your hair?

Maybe this Liesel was a maniac. Maybe she was a serial killer hiding out in Cardiff or Swansea. Maybe there was a reason her family had not accompanied her to Cuba. Maybe they had not been seen in some time.

Clare argued that Bryony was not remembering properly, that everything was just the same. Bryony pointed a plump finger and told Clare that something was not right here; something was not right with *her*. She inhaled, as though she was about to keep going, and then stopped herself. The recognition of the problem seemed to be enough. She was not compelled to solve it. She turned away and sailed into the vast room, her broad red shoulders swinging. Clare imagined Bryony, in the days to come, talking to a colleague who had been on the trip with Liesel, a colleague who also said her name like a sigh and had seen the photos of her family. Bryony would describe seeing Liesel again, in Havana, and how different she seemed—how peculiar and erratic and vague. Something different about her hair too. A change that did not become her.

Any more sun and that woman is going to need emergency services, Arlo said as he watched her go. So how many names do you have?

The movie screen went dark and people began to flood the landing; she thought that if she stayed very still it would only be a matter of time before she was carried away. Clare was a little disappointed at how quickly Arlo had abandoned their collusion. She had wanted to keep pretending. When she told him there had been a case of confused identity, he said Bryony wasn't the only person getting too much sun.

Clare woke with an irrepressible desire to go to the zoo. The zoo, the zoo, the zoo, she said as she washed her face in the round bathroom sink, flecks of hair still clinging to the drain. She had not succeeded in finding Richard on the street or in the cemetery or at the festival, which would soon enter its final weeks—why not try the zoo? The brochure had migrated to the bedside table, and she imagined the tiger implanting ideas into her mind while she slept.

In the taxi, the driver listened to opera; at stop lights he conducted the air. The car was large as a hearse with floral upholstery and no seat belts, a small fire extinguisher fastened behind the driver's seat. At the zoo, she was delivered into a series of lines: one to get in; one to buy tickets; one to board the slumping red Girón buses that carted visitors around the park.

Tomorrow she would leave for the airport, tomorrow she would board a plane. The more she repeated *tomorrow* to herself the more the word sounded fictional, though she supposed all words were fictional in the sense that someone had invented them.

At the zoo, the lines moved slowly. Richard had, in his former life, hated lines.

The brochure detailed the recent overhaul the zoo had undergone, which included importing one hundred and fifty wild animals from Namibia. The project was nicknamed Noah's Ark and the imported animals included a dozen baby rhinos and five elephants and a rare kind of crocodile. How did you get five elephants on a plane? The brochure declined to detail the logistics; rather, the reader's attention was directed to other refurbishments. To the new fencing and resurfaced paths and the lion enclosure and the crocodile pit and the flamingo pool—all paid for with government money. The staff had received special training in the care of the Namibian animals. A breeding program had been established, with a focus on making more rare crocodiles. This zoo was part of the new Cuba now.

In the ticket line, she kept wondering what it must have been like for those animals to wake up one day and find themselves in Havana.

On the bus, Clare was the only single party. Everyone else was part of a family. She sat near the front, in a window seat, a child next to her, an American boy with a mop of coppery hair going on about renting a scooter. When could he ride a scooter? What colors did they come in? How fast did they go? When could he ride one? When? His parents were sitting directly in front of him. They did not acknowledge the boy and she would not have believed they were his parents at all if the mother didn't have the same sharp chin, the father the same coppery hair.

Oh, the thin line between love and exhaustion. The thin line between love and indifference. The thin line between I Am Like a Little Boat Cut Loose in a Storm Without You and You Are Driving Me Rapidly Insane.

The engine roared. Her seat shuddered and she struggled to hear the driver, who was also the guide. He wore an olive uniform. His voice was being inhaled by a black microphone. The first pen, the ostrich pen, was empty, because yesterday a sinkhole had decimated a key stretch of fencing, creating an opening through which three ostriches had fled. Apparently these ostriches had already been spotted outside the Hotel Bella Habana and in the Colon Cemetery. The driver warned the passengers against approaching a loose ostrich, should they see one, as they could kick you hard enough to kill you.

Next the bus stopped at the lion enclosure, a dilapidated cinder-block palace ringed by a moat of foamy green. The lions—some sleek as housecats, some with huge russet manes—stalked their terrain in the same lethally methodical manner as a killer. The guide, now shouting into the microphone, advised the passengers to keep the windows rolled up. A couple in panama hats fake-screamed for a selfie. Clare wondered if Yuniel Mata had considered filming a scene in this zoo.

The guide said something Clare couldn't catch over the engine, and the mother sitting in front of her cried out, Horsemeat! then looked at the skulking lions with dismay. She bit her knuckles. Her child kicked the back of her seat. The bus lurched down a winding, forested path and they emerged to find hippos chest-deep in mud and zebras trotting across a brown field, tails switching, and later sunset-colored flamingos highstepping through an emerald pool shielded by palm trees. She watched one flamingo crane its neck, as though composing a thought, and dunk its head into the water.

They ended at the crocodile pit, where those prehistoric beasts were sunning themselves on concrete slabs. These crocodiles were twice the size of regular alligators, snouts as long and narrow as the barrel of a gun, scales shining like they had been basted in oil. She asked the guide to point out the rare crocodiles and got an unintelligible reply. Maybe this crocodile-breeding program was a sham. They were moving on from the pit when a man in a baseball cap shouted, Look! and they all turned in time to see crocodiles slipping into the water and rushing toward a common point. There was a slash of bright yellow—feathers, a strangled squawk, a bird of some kind—and then the crocodiles lunged and the feathered thing vanished underwater. The boy sitting beside Clare stopped kicking his mother's seat and cried out, with unmistakable delight, They're killing it! They're killing it!

At dawn, her period struck and she bled all over the hotel sheets (that was how it happened now, in her later thirties: a sudden, stabbing pain, blood like a crime scene, a furious reminder that in the eyes of culture and nature her body was inching ever closer to uselessness). She could not stand the thought of Isa or a total stranger discovering all that blood. She peeled off her pajamas, stripped the bed, and dumped the linens in the bathtub. She would erase the evidence; no misdeed had been committed here.

She crouched in the back of the tub. She held the linens under the tap and watched the bloody water rush down the drain. She nudged the loose molar with her tongue. She cupped water in her hands and cleaned herself. She imagined the eel had been sliced open, that it had bled out inside her.

She dressed and hung the sheets over the balcony to dry. She listened to motorbikes rip through the newly born morning. She felt shocked back into time.

In the building across the street, an arched window blazed with light. Clare fetched her binoculars and made out a woman in a kitchen, washing dishes. She was wearing pink gloves that rose to her elbows. For a moment, the woman glanced up and Clare wondered if she sensed she was being watched.

The woman vanished from the kitchen. The light in the window went out. Clare imagined her getting back into bed still wearing those pink gloves.

Later she folded the towels in the bathroom, tossed the trash into the trash, closed all the drawers. A small part of her would forever open a hotel room drawer expecting a fingernail. She kneeled and patted the space underneath the bed, to make sure she wasn't leaving anything behind, and felt a hole in the floor. With each of these acts, a voice inside her roared, *home*. In the bathroom, she brushed her hair smooth and straight, and told herself she looked just as she did when she arrived.

At the front desk, Isa, in a white T-shirt with DESIGN spelled out in black sequins, snapped her astronomy textbook shut and asked Clare if she was leaving any magazines. Apparently the last American woman traveling alone had left behind a stack of *Us Weekly*.

Clare unzipped her backpack and took out *The Two Faces of January*. She slid the paperback across the desk.

I finished it last night, she said. You can have it if you want.

She had brought the book all the way with her to Havana and had not read a single word. She recalled an article about how people told three times as many lies when they were away from home, a figure that had struck her as low.

Isa picked up the book, started reading the back copy. On the cover, a man in a suit and a fedora stood in the shadows of a Greek ruin. She told Clare that she had taught herself to read novels in English by translating the mysteries left behind by the British and American and Canadian guests.

I should be tired of mysteries by now, she said. I've never read one set in Greece.

José Martí International, Clare said to the taxi driver. A small, stuffed bear hung from the rearview. A medical license was taped to the dashboard.

The terminal Clare was deposited into was far more up-to-date than the terminal she had arrived at. Here there was ample seating, efficient security, shops, cafés. It was a different world, this terminal. How did she get here?

Her flight was on time.

At customs, she handed over her exit papers and stared into the camera until her photo had been recorded. The moment she reached the other side of security the inner voice that had cried out *home* began to soften.

She ignored this softening. She stalked past the duty-free and the souvenir shops and the stall selling Wi-Fi and the mustard-and-white currency exchange bureau. She went into the bathroom, where two ticket agents were smoking, standing side by side and gusting into the mirror. If her husband were here, he would have called this an interior zone of vulnerability, where public and private smash together. What could be more intimate than listening to a stranger take a difficult shit? Yet this zone depended on silence. The intimacy was to be felt but never admitted. To admit would violate the rules. Another urban horror film he had been studying for his book took place exclusively in an apartment building in Barcelona, in interior zones of vulnerability, in hallways and bathrooms and elevators.

She followed a sign for coffee down a flight of stairs. She waited in line behind a man toting a plastic doll the height of a child, bound in Saran wrap and standing upright in a shopping bag. The doll was facing her, eyes open and horrible through the plastic. Clare sneezed and a familiar voice called out, Bless you! She spun around and there was Davi, leaning against a red cement pillar and smiling wide, his duffel bag at his feet, black headphones looped around his neck. All the major films had screened during the festival's first week, so he was heading home. What luck, his smile seemed to say. What luck to meet on the plane and find each other again at the airport. The circle had been closed.

They sat together at a table, Clare facing the stairs. A brown-and-white spaniel in a faded K9 vest lay at the bottom, keeping a listless watch. Their coffees had been served in white china with pink flowers, the cup and saucer so tiny she could not help but think they had been designed for the hands of a child.

This airport will be renovated before long, Davi said. A French architecture firm got the job. Can't happen soon enough. He added that soon there would be better hotels to look forward to as well: a Swiss company was bringing the first five-star hotel to Havana, in partnership with Gaviota. There was to be a massive spa and five different restaurants and a luxury shopping mall. The hotel would be constructed by the same French architecture firm tasked with renovating the airport. Foreign money and foreign labor, so much for anticapitalism, and it wouldn't do fuck all for anyone who lived here—apart, he supposed, from attracting more tourists, the benefits of which were debatable.

But if you come back, you'll know where to get a good Swiss massage, Davi said, raising his cup. Am I right to think that you wouldn't complain?

Near Parque Central, Clare had passed the hotel site rising from the ground, the scaffolding looming over the surrounding buildings; one afternoon she had spotted two teenage girls in school uniforms taking a selfie by the structure. In airplane magazines, she had seen advertisements from this same hotel group that featured a woman in a snug black hospitality uniform holding a tray with a bourbon on the rocks, her mouth a red lacquered O, ready to serve.

What will happen when you go home? she asked, because she was truly uncertain what would happen when she went home. She thought of the empty condominium in New Scotland. Through a window she glimpsed a plane ascending into a cloudless sky. She thought of her father's voice on the phone, and the glass trembled.

What will happen? Davi sipped his coffee. Deadlines, deadlines, deadlines. The films out of Colombia will be the big story. Buying my girlfriend something so perfect and lovely for Christmas she'll forget she's mad at me for traveling all year. When she's angry, she tells me to go stand in front of the mirror and ask myself if I see the center of the world looking back.

He shook his head and laughed, acquiring the air of someone accustomed to being out of favor with the women in his life, but he could afford this disfavor because he always knew the way back in.

For Christmas, she would be expected in Florida. There would be recipes to cook and wreaths to hang and gifts to buy. She had spent Thanksgiving in a hotel room in Lincoln. At a gas station, she'd bought two packets of an off-brand sleep aid—enough to pull her under. She'd woke feeling like she'd been up all night. Her mother had wanted her to come to Florida; Clare had claimed the trip to Nebraska was unavoidable. At this moment there were far fewer miles between them than when Clare was in New York.

A trip to visit family in Olinda, Davi continued. Maybe a little time by the sea. And you?

By the stairs the spaniel barked. A woman in a khaki skirt suit and a tangerine scarf, the uniform of a security officer, appeared. She unleashed the spaniel, plucked a blue rubber ball from her pocket. She tossed the ball and the spaniel dove after it.

Clare would find a way to live full-time on an airplane. She would forget her father was dying. She would forget she had ever seen her husband here, had allowed her reality to become so dislocated, had fallen into the age-old tourist trap of arriving in a place and projecting the thing she wanted most in the world onto a screen.

Work, she said.

Davi raised an eyebrow. And?

A security camera was mounted on the red pillar. Her husband once said horror films often started by plunging the viewer into the sight of the killer—heavy footsteps in the woods, a gloved hand clutching a knife—because when you see as they see, when you watch the victim transform from person to object, you are thrilled and then you are implicated. She stared into the lens and tried to turn herself into an object, a sight. She tried to imagine the killer telling her that it was time to go, that soon her flight would leave and when it did she would be on it, her nose pressed to the oval window.

There is no *and*, she wanted to tell Davi.

Or, at least not an *and* that she could name.

The softening turned into a melting, an avalanche.

Work, she said again.

Clare felt something spring across her feet and then the spaniel was diving under the table, its fur brushing her shins. The dog snapped up the ball and trotted back to the woman with the tangerine scarf, tail erect, proud.

She overturned her tiny cup and coffee rushed across the table, dripping onto Davi's slacks. For a moment, she did nothing but watch the liquid stream down.

Christ, I'm sorry, she said after she snapped to, mopping at the table and then his knee with a paper napkin, flushed and clumsy.

The dog, the dog, he said, waving her away. He excused himself to the bathroom. The woman in the tangerine scarf leashed the spaniel and began to lead him around like a show dog, to the delight of the waiting children.

See the green fields laced with fog. See the city turn miniature. See the great blue yawn of the sea.

Or.

She rose from her seat. She gathered her bags.

Davi had been wrong. The circle was not closed.

The circle was not closed because she was going to break it.

On her way back to Vedado, Clare devised her lie: a canceled flight; an indefinite departure date, given the peak season. She could almost hear the obfuscating language of a customer service representative, language designed to strip the speaker of all agency and accountability. *A problem has arisen. This system does not have any more information for you right now.* Language she had used herself when something went awry in the world of elevators.

At the Third Hotel, the German college student was at the front desk, asking Isa questions about the schedule for the Viazul

Bus to Varadero. Before leaving he tucked another pink carnation into the plastic cup serving as a penholder. When Isa saw Clare in the doorway, she placed a white coffee mug on top of *The Two Faces of January* and gave her a long look. Clare made a mental note to e-mail her boss with the news that a problem with her flight had forced an extended stay.

In the room, she returned her passport and the white box to the safe. She was very nearly out of pesos and the line for the exchange counter at the airport would have taken hours, so she had walked from the terminal to the nearest bus stop, along a roadside not so unlike the one Richard had been walking when he was struck. Traffic trickled by at a comfortable speed and then a fleet of tour buses screamed past and she leapt into a ditch. In Havana, she had disembarked at the first stop that looked familiar, though it would turn out the intersection she thought was familiar was, in fact, not—and so she had wandered for some time, half lost, before finding her way back to Vedado. From the Third Hotel, the closest CADECA was on La Rampa, on a street corner shaded by a banana tree, the roots cracking up through the concrete like claws. She fell into the back of a long line.

When she reached the front, the man behind the window would not exchange her money because she had neglected to bring her passport, required for government records. She went back to the Third Hotel, retrieved her passport, and returned to the CADECA—delighted to find that the line had evaporated until she realized that was only because the window had closed for the day.

And then, at the corner of La Rampa and Calle M, there was Richard, buying a mango from a fruit cart hitched to a blue bicycle. The sidewalk trembled. Heat traveled upward through the concrete and the soles of her shoes, stunning her immobile. The mental note to write to her boss fluttered away. The tear in her own atmosphere widened. This time, Clare told herself that she would not repeat her past mistakes. She would not approach him. She would not use the name he had once gone by, the name she had forced herself to stop saying. Those old signifiers did not mean anything to him here.

She stayed on the opposite side of the street until her husband carried the mango away in a brown paper bag. She darted across, ignoring the traffic signals, and trailed behind him. She was covert, allowing pedestrians to drift between. It was hot, and each person she passed on the street seemed to be emitting a slight glow.

A pair of long-backed dogs trotted away from tourists armed with cameras, disinterested in being turned into subjects. Clare was terrified to take a photo—that the brief freezing of time would shatter whatever reality she had slipped down into, that she would look up and find Richard was no longer there, the anguish of having chosen an image of a person over the person himself.

For a block, there was no one between them. She could see the shapes of his legs moving inside his pants. She wondered if she had become telekinetic, like in *Carrie*, if her grief was so overwhelming she had acquired the ability to conjure her husband whenever she wished to see him, though if that were true it seemed like she should be able to conjure him right into stillness.

They passed the Meliá Cohiba hotel and the newly reopened American embassy. Outside the embassy the American flag had been raised; Clare could not say that she ever felt particularly happy to see her own flag. They crossed an iron bridge spanning a still river and then she was in a part of the city she had never seen before. They moved up a broad avenida, divided by a green mall. They passed foreign embassies—Italy, Switzerland, Angola—identified by the guard booths outside, occupied by somber men in mirrored glasses. They passed a grand house with a gleaming car in a gated driveway, a life-size plastic Santa standing by the hubcap like a valet. Two shaggy goldens stuck their snouts through the bars, barking as she passed. A park with a round white pantheon, the dome in the process of being consumed by green moss, and massive, ancient banyan trees.

They turned down a street, past a café with a tile patio covered by midnight-blue umbrellas. Avenida Thirty-Two, Avenida Thirty-Six; they were rising and rising. She followed him along one uneven street and around a corner and then along another, the sidewalk crumbling at the edges. There were few pedestrians, so she had to hang back, and from behind a palm tree she watched him stop in front of an aquamarine building surrounded by green chain-link fencing, the entrance shrouded by an overgrown yard. She counted a boat lily and needle palms and yellow hibiscuses and a verdant lime tree. Two rocking chairs stood outside the door, unoccupied and swaying in the warm wind. For a moment, he stood on the sidewalk, holding the paper bag in one hand, as though assessing the mango's weight, and then he passed through the gate and the yard swallowed him.

A moment later, a light in a room facing an alleyway came on.

The fence was waist-high, low enough for her to jump. In the alley, she flung herself over, landing in a heap in the grass. She kneeled by the window and peered into a simple room with a bed, a small table, a single chair. No sign of a TV. She noticed a black-and-white cat in the corner, and it took her a mo-

ment to understand that the cat was not real but a ceramic rep-
lica. Above the bed a framed cross-stitch read, in Spanish, God
Bless Our Home.

She watched as Richard sat at the table. He smoothed the
paper bag into a place mat and used a small knife to peel the
mango skin. He ate the fruit in glistening slivers the color of
sunshine. When he was finished, he took out a slim book. She
couldn't make out the title, but it was not anything like the
thick academic texts he once read. More like a play or a book
of poetry. He held this mysterious book with one hand, his left
hand; with his right he cupped his elbow. He licked his lips.
Every so often he rubbed the toe of his shoe against the floor, in
the manner of someone slowly extinguishing a cigarette. She
noticed every movement. She was certain she had never noticed him so thoroughly. Radically alert and radically alive
and why on earth had she waited so long to pay this kind of
attention.

All around she could feel the city darken as night drew in,
but she was mesmerized by how the room seemed to grow
brighter and brighter. Where was all that light coming from?
She should have felt pain in her knees and in her back, but she
did not; her body was fused to the earth. She watched him turn
page after page, looking for some kind of useful clue, and then
she was ashamed to realize she had missed the most obvious
clue of all. She dared to let her nose touch the glass. She dared
to let her breath fog the pane. She was so close. She felt a boil-
ing in her stomach.

In this room, there was indeed a table with a round face and
four solid legs, not so unlike their kitchen table in New Scotland, except here there was only one chair. In their kitchen,
there were always two chairs—never three, never five, never

zero, never one. Always two. A single chair suggested solitude. There was no expectation of hosting dinners with friends or out-of-town guests or a woman who sometimes spent the night. You were your own company.

In this life, he was alone.

PART 2

MORBID URGES

Another film her husband had been writing about for his book was a French movie about people who simply came back. These returned people had died, funerals had been held in their names, and now they were appearing in the city center, clothed and in fine health. At first, they were divided by age and gender and temporarily housed in airplane hangars. Families had to provide papers and passports and photos to claim their undead. In this movie, there was no blood, no biting and lurching. The undead had the vestiges of their former memories; their body temperatures were five degrees lower; they pretended to sleep at night but they were faking, none of them actually slept. They all looked serene and terrified. A doctor theorized they were stuck in a latent period, still in the process of awakening into a new life, though in the end the doctor concluded this latent period would be unending. Meanwhile, the undead experienced an unspoken and collective realization of their own: suddenly they were driven to leave their families, to roam out into the countryside. They were drawn to underground places, down into sewers and tunnels. In one scene, a man's undead wife tried to climb a garden wall, in order to escape their home. The man ran out into the yard in his pajamas, his bare feet a luminescent white in the green grass. He shouted her name. She climbed faster. He grabbed hold of her ankle. When she turned to look at him, her expression suggested it was not her undead state that was so strange; rather, it was the state of the living—a state so starved and selfish it was willing to make her a prisoner, if that's what it took to keep her close—that was the most deranged one of all.

The *where* was nowhere and maybe the *here* was nowhere too.

The deepest pleasure of the zombie story lies always in its depiction of the break, that exhilarating moment of long-hoped-for upheaval: the fulfillment of a sometimes avowed, sometimes disavowed, desire to see power at last unmade, laid finally to waste and torn limb from limb—and our structures of dominion and domination replaced finally and forever with Utopia, if only for the already dead. —Gerry Canavan. Page twenty-seven, paragraph two, discovered in a black leather notebook while Clare was cleaning out Richard's home office, the upper right-hand corner lacquered with a brown half circle of coffee.

In Richard's office, sitting cross-legged on the floor, she had kept reading about zombies until she found a small manila envelope, her name on the front, her parents' address in the return field, tucked inside the pages. The envelope held a notebook, small and red. She had opened this little notebook and then closed it just as quickly, feeling like she had been slapped. She dropped both notebooks into a file cabinet drawer and rushed from the office, upsetting a chair, leaving the desk lamp ablaze. A gold triangle shot out the bottom of the door for three days and then the light extinguished itself.

What if that's what happened? Clare thought as she wandered the festival hotel. What if he just came back? That afternoon, and the afternoon before, she had crossed the iron bridge into Miramar, where she had observed her husband drinking cafe-citos on the café patio, in the shade of a midnight-blue umbrella. He read the newspaper. He did not speak to anyone. Both times, she noticed a diminutive man in a black suit sitting at a table nearby; he had a flaxseed mustache, too heavy for his face. He spoke Spanish with an American accent. Perhaps he was a diplomat, given the volume of embassies in Miramar. After Richard left the café, she'd trailed her husband to the fruit market, where he bought vast quantities of mangoes. She never saw him report to a job or greet another person on the street. In this life, he appeared to be a man of leisure. At exactly two in the afternoon, he disappeared into a hospital by the river for an hour; at nightfall, he drank at a bar overlooking a small park, this one absent of banyan trees. In the back of her guidebook, she had logged the details of every sighting. She had always imagined herself to be the kind of person who passed unnoticed through airports and hotels, a white woman of middling age and appearance, in tan pantsuits and unfashionable pumps. A luxury, this ability to slip through unseen, and she was putting it to use.

One of the festival theaters, Cine Karl Marx, was in Miramar. When she noticed that *Revolución Zombi* was showing, she'd felt the theater doors gust open, draw her inside.

On second viewing, it did seem true that the undead could unmake power. They could do what the living could not. There was nothing they could not overthrow. If the citizens had tried to unmake power, they would have been arrested and interrogated and thrown in jail, but there was no arresting these zombies or throwing them in jail. They were free to rage and rage.

Her husband had believed that once the theater went dark and the film began, the viewer was alone—even if they had arrived in the company of others. This solitude was needed to dissolve the logic and laws of the world they had come from, replacing those principles with the logic and laws of the screen; that was how Yuniel Mata's eels slipped past. In this way you could descend into the theater with a person you knew intimately and then, once the lights returned, find yourself seated next to a stranger.

She stopped at the edge of the hotel terrace, looked out at the churning sea. Behind every death lay a set of questions. To *move on* was to agree to not disturb these questions, to let them settle with the body under the earth. Yet some questions so thoroughly dismantled the terms of your own life, turning away was gravitationally impossible. So she would not be moving on. She would keep disturbing and disturbing. She imagined herself standing over a grave with a shovel and hacking away at the soil.

Clare glimpsed a woman hurrying down the Malecón, in the direction of the Anti-Imperialist Plaza; even from a distance, she recognized those precise shoulders. She removed her binoculars from her backpack, raised the round lenses to her face. Agata Alonso's hair was different—short and black this time, with severe bangs, like a twenties film star. She was carrying a round case. Red, Clare observed, and perhaps made of leather. Where could she be going?

Clare had gotten stuck in an elevator exactly once in her life, in a doll factory in Heltonville, Indiana. The cables malfunctioned, suspending the car between floors. She was with the foreman, who had been explaining the process of making doll heads, when they stalled. Apart from his fascination with doll heads, he had appeared entirely normal.

They had pressed the alarm button and reached emergency services; after that, nothing to do but wait. In an in-flight magazine she'd once read the quietest place on earth was an anechoic chamber in Minnesota. The longest anyone had ever lasted in there was forty-five minutes, and she was certain she would not fare any better.

In the elevator, the silence made her arms itch and she was relieved when the foreman broke it, until he informed her that he had just observed her soul leaving her body. Apparently souls left bodies *all* the time—what entity didn't need a break every now and again? He believed this was only a problem if the soul in question lacked a reason to return. He explained that he had seen her soul climb right out of her chest—he stepped forward and pressed a freckled hand against her clavicle—and perch like a gargoyle on her shoulders, and when it was clear that she was utterly oblivious to what was transpiring, well—

The foreman sighed and shrugged, as though the departure of a soul was a terrible shame, but a situation for which there was little recourse. She told him she was under the assumption that souls only left bodies when people died, and he began to laugh and—his tone pivoting to indicate this was among the more idiotic things he'd heard in his life—said, You think *that's* what happens when people die? He shook his head and stared up at the ceiling hatch, which opened not long after, the hands of their rescuers reaching down.

That night, in Heltonville, she had the impulse to weigh herself in the hotel gym: she had lost three pounds overnight. She was pretty sure the soul was supposed to weigh less than three pounds, that it was perhaps without physical weight, but nevertheless she felt chilled. The next day she was scheduled to return to the factory, but instead she took a derelict drive through the countryside, comforted by the heft of the land.

The foreman had been possessed by a completely different notion of how the spiritual realm operated and he had spoken about it with a confidence that seemed preposterous in the moment, but who could say for sure that he was wrong, that the empty drift that gripped some people at certain moments in life was *not* in fact due to their souls—perhaps temporarily, perhaps permanently—abandoning their bodies.

No one, that was who.

At the Third Hotel, she called her mother and learned of her father's new habit of wandering from the house, front door swung open, and getting lost in the neighborhood. Her mother would find him in the middle of the street or stumbling through a backyard, swatting at bushes, dog shit stuck to his heels. A plump male Bobtail had slipped out last week and had not been seen since. Her father had many months ahead, but they would not be good ones.

I hate to think about what's happened to the cat, her mother said. Torn to bits by wild animals. Run down by a car.

The line went silent. Her mother cleared her throat.

Sorry, she said. I shouldn't have mentioned the car.

In the dawn of her father's illness, back when he was cheerfully muddled and easily returned to the center, the anger that had always coursed through her parents' home had eased. She'd glimpsed them holding hands in the backyard or watching a movie on the sofa, etched in a tenderness rarely witnessed in health. Now that his confusion was no longer gentle, now that it was full of resistance, the high-voltage fury had returned— the fury that had left Clare wanting to feel as little as possible, to press an ice cube against her heart.

At the Seahorse, their marriage had been like a stationary storm hunkered down on an unfortunate slice of coast, battering the land. They'd retired five years ago, moving out of the attached apartment Clare had been raised in and into a ranch-style near Ponte Vedra, but it was too late for them to change. The storm was the only weather system they knew, and systems in general were very hard to shed.

The guests, on the other hand, had been transitory. Clare did not consider the private storms they might be stuck inside, not even when she spotted them moving through the open-air halls with the skittish heaviness of a person being stalked by something inevitable and awful. Stay in motion, she had instructed herself, and escape the storm.

Movement.

On the phone, her mother switched over to Christmas: who would be there, what they would bring. She was too tired to make her famed cloudberry cake this year. All those layers of cream and jam. How Clare's father had decided that celebrities were being replaced by clones, so best to not watch any movies. How she knew her daughter was in a hard stretch right now. She remembered what it was like when her parents died; sometimes the pain was so splitting she thought she would go blind. It was brutal, the mortality contract. It came for everyone and no one was prepared. How everyone would miss Richard this year. She would not be alone in that missing.

You won't be alone, her mother repeated, but Clare could not hear her. She had already placed the phone on the bed and walked away.

Later, she woke up on the bathroom floor, as she had started falling asleep in places that were not her bed. On the toilet, in the chair next to the dresser.

She kept the box locked up in the safe.

That night, Clare dreamed she was living in the future and in this future no one went anywhere anymore. Rather, they traveled—if you could call it that—through holograms that projected the place they desired straight into their homes. The trick, though, was that the hologram not only projected the place but what the traveler wished to experience there—spiritual absolution while rock climbing in the Alps, say. Finally the age-old quest for authenticity had been quelled, for what was this quest but a desire to be carried far away from yourself, to escape the borders of your own identity. To lie and have the lie feel real. On the terrace of the festival hotel, the American man had said, Wasn't she glad they had come when they had? Before this became yet another place that only brought us back to ourselves? This desire to escape one's country, and one's countrypeople, was greatest in those who came from empires, which were designed to be inescapable. Citizens could find traces of the empire nearly everywhere they went, and when there was no evidence to be found, they manifested it—for to be a citizen of an empire meant to also be a kind of carrier. With this system of holograms, travel could be initiated at any time, without ever leaving your home. And so, from her bedroom in New Scotland, Clare strolled through the old part of Havana until she happened upon her husband standing outside the Museum of the Revolution.

We are not yet finished with each other, she had told him in the dream.

In the morning, she set out to visit the sites used for scenes in *Revolución Zombi,* or at least the ones she had been able to recognize. She took notes in her guidebook. Maybe she really could be a film critic, drafting her piece. Perhaps she would write about the spatial qualities of the film, in relation to urban horror. A city was not meant to be empty—a city devoid of inhabitants was an unwell city, a thing to be feared. A city was to be peopled and but not *too* peopled—a city overcome (by, say, a zombie horde) was equally fearsome. Yuniel Mata's film had been the most frightening when the city appeared empty, the unexamined quarters lying in wait, or when it was overrun, when the inhabitants of those hidden quarters rose up and demanded to be counted. She imagined her husband would consider these observations rudimentary, but she had to start somewhere.

After another visit to the Malecón and Plaza de la Revolución and Parque Central, where the luxury hotel was rising, she broke for a coffee on Avenida Lamparilla. She was sitting outside, in a wagon wheel of shade, when she saw Arlo on the sidewalk. He was carrying a rectangular cardboard box, the kind that might contain a small cake. She called his name and waved, inviting him to join her.

What's in the box? she asked.

Nothing exciting. He sat down and slid the box under his chair, out of sight. I'm on an errand for the festival.

A waiter came by and Arlo ordered a beer. His badge was tucked under his T-shirt, but she could see the plastic square pressing against the cotton and the black lanyard curving around his neck.

I've noticed you're left-handed, he said.

He picked up a spoon and tapped her lightly on the back of her hand.

My father says that if you're left-handed it's because once another infant lived in the womb with you, but you absorbed your twin and during that process everything about you became inverted. My father calls left-handed people twin-eaters. He says he wishes I had thought to absorb my sister when we were still in the womb.

They were seated across from a building with a mural of a woman's face, her hair a violet rope. A window opened, making a hollow space in the side of her head. Nearby a small white dog was curled tight under a streetlight, sleeping off the heat, the fur under its eyes stained copper.

What are you writing? He nodded toward the open guidebook, the uncapped pen. When she told him she was writing about Yuniel Mata's film, Arlo snorted.

Horror claims to scare audiences, he said, when in fact it does just the opposite.

I scare easy then, Clare said. She shivered every time she thought of Yuniel Mata's eels.

Arlo went on to say that people entered into a horror film expecting to be unsettled, which made a true unsettling near impossible, as a true unsettling could not be seen coming. The screaming was only pleasurable because the audience knew the terror had an end. Their fear was a commodity—fake and disposable. These qualities were, of course, what made the genre so profitable.

Clare supposed this perspective shouldn't come as a surprise given that Arlo was a documentarian. Her husband had once written that the ideal film existed between consciousness and unconsciousness, and it seemed to her that this was the true terrain of horror—it was the genre of the liminal, the in-between.

She pointed out that any image could be manipulated, and that perhaps horror was just a very specific kind of manipulation, and Arlo replied that to film was to manipulate, the two acts could not be separated. There was nothing neutral about the lens, but the director's aim should be to thin the membrane between the world of the viewer and the world of the screen. He quoted a Russian critic on the "shock of veracity" and said that he had no interest in seeing a film set in, say, the countryside if he did not leave the theater feeling as though he could taste the dirt on his skin. Horror, he continued, had the opposite goal. To bathe the reader in blood until they felt safe, to thicken the membrane.

Documentary, on the other hand, Arlo said, documentary is the genre of persuasion.

Now you have plans for a documentary on light fixtures or a documentary on suicides, Clare said. Which one is it?

Who says the two subjects are unrelated?

I don't see the connection myself, Clare said. Maybe you could explain?

Arlo replied that if the relationship between the two could be explained in a café then he would not need to make a film.

Americans like straight answers, Clare said, intending to make a joke of her national character. We like simple stories.

Her own vast and incurious country often felt alien to her, with its unimaginative pledges and toxic patriotism, its aversion to discomfort and complex thought (the death of her brother-in-law alone had been enough to instill in her a hatred of truisms—what was so impossible about saying, Right now our lives are *fucked up* and we don't know exactly when things will get better?), its desire to be recognized as a beacon of justice without ever actually acting like one. At the same time, America was the only country she had ever lived in, and she understood it could be disingenuous, perhaps even dangerous, to allow herself to feel superior to the thing she had always lived inside, the thing that had made her.

A Spanish family settled in next to them. The mother fanned herself with a menu, surrounded by three hot and uninterested teenage boys—all several heads taller than she.

Where are you from in America? he said next. I never asked.

Already she had told people she was from New York and was met with disappointment when they realized she meant upstate and not the City. When she tried Florida, she was met with disappointment when they realized she meant North Florida and that she knew little of Miami. This time, she did not hesitate.

I'm from Nebraska.

And what is Nebraska like?

You want me to describe Nebraska?

Yes, he said. Tell me a simple story about Nebraska.

She had never been asked to describe Nebraska before, and now that the occasion had arrived she felt ill-equipped. Her travel schedule had been like a migratory pattern, a loop of hotels and airports and offices, little room for unmediated contact. She had met plenty of people who lived in Nebraska, but their conversations rarely strayed from elevators. She could, however, describe in vivid detail the smell of a certain hotel carpet in Lincoln. In Illinois, a strip of highway that she called World's Largest: you'd pass signs for the world's largest golf tee and wind chime and rocking chair. In a pinch, she had used credit cards and shoe heels to scrape ice off windshields. She had an internalized ranking of airport restaurants and bars. She knew the transient circuits of these places with intimacy, and even when these circuits were interrupted by weather or mechanical problems or a missing flight crew or a bomb threat, she knew the contingency plans. What lay outside those circuits, however, was a foreign land.

A different America, she had told Richard many times over.

Yet she had never investigated; her own country's incuriosity had infected her.

Arlo's beer arrived. He took a drink.

Well? he said.

She began with the cornfields. The movement of the corn in the wind could be as beautiful as anything else on this earth. There were sunflower and wheat fields too. Silver grain silos dotted some of these fields like oversize bullets. Sorrel horses with rumps pressed against rounds of hay. There were prairies and dunes, depending on which part of the state you were in. She found the cities hunched and gray. The winters were very cold.

I'll pass, said Arlo.

She picked up her coffee.

I love Nebraska. It's a beautiful place.

If Nebraska is so beautiful, Arlo said, then what are you still doing here?

The ceramic handle went hot on her skin. She put her coffee back down so quickly the cup rattled, nearly tipped.

In the days after she abandoned her flight, she had considered the absence of her body on the plane, the absence of her face pressed to the window and her stampeding mind thinking desperate thoughts about the pilot's intentions. The absence of the life where she did not break the circle, where she defied gravity and turned away.

My husband is here, she said.

Saying the words aloud made her feel like her head had been lifted clean from her body.

Arlo leaned forward, eyebrows raised, like she had just uttered something mildly obscene. He made a steeple with his hands. Your husband is *where*?

She told him that Richard was here, in Havana, and that she knew this was the first time she'd ever mentioned her husband, mentioned being married at all, and that she must sound very strange right now. Arlo turned his beer on the table. He started to say something but stopped short. A pause was a gap; too many in a conversation and the gap would widen into a canyon. Perhaps he thought she was playing another game, like the one where she had pretended to be a woman named Liesel.

He finished his beer. He picked up the box and rose from his chair. He held it gingerly, with flat palms. Clare felt certain something delicate or dangerous sat inside. He stepped out of the wagon wheel of shade, a safe distance away. He looked her up and down and told her to not take what he was about to say next the wrong way. Or be offended. What did he care. But, if she was serious about her husband, she might want to consider a dress.

The following morning Clare took a long, cool bath. The tub was short and she kept her legs bent. She stared down at the small pouch of belly, the tangle between her thighs. Sometimes she liked to pet that dark tangle and imagine she was alive at a different moment in history. She shaved her legs and underarms. She followed Arlo's advice and zipped herself into the only dress she packed, a yellow eyelet sundress with cap sleeves. The hemline fell midcalf, a small mercy, for she'd always believed herself to have ugly knees—plus thick wrists and a fat purple vein that bulged around her left anklebone; sometimes she thought it looked like it was going to break through the skin. She scrubbed the dirt lines from her fingernails. She rubbed lotion into her cheeks.

In Plaza de Armas, she bought *The Collected Poems of Hart Crane*. She walked back into Vedado and then followed Linea all the way to the art factory, teeming at night and shuttered during the day, the entire block quiet.

She stepped slowly across the river. She did not feel quite like herself.

In Miramar, she went straight to the café, the small sea of midnight-blue umbrellas. Richard was there, reading the newspaper. She took note of the items arranged on the table: the silver pitcher of cream, the blue sugar bowl, the discarded sections of the paper. No detail could go unnoticed, even if he did not yet notice her, did not so much as glance up when she appeared on the patio in her eyelet dress, her fingernails clean, her cheeks fiery with lotion and sweat.

She sat at the table next to him, in a bamboo chair. She opened the book. She read a line about the fabulous shadow the sea keeps and found the notion exquisite, the shadow the sea keeps, and wondered if she should start reading more poetry.

A waiter came by, and she ordered a café con leche and a flan. On the opposite side of the patio, two women were arguing in French. Clare was not close enough to make out the particulars. They were facing each other, long, bronzed legs sticking out like spears. One woman smacked the table and a little dish fell, casting white splinters across the tile. The suited man with the flaxseed mustache stepped onto the patio, a newspaper tucked under his arm, and selected a table near the arguing women. Up close she could see his thin, downturned mouth; he had her father's high forehead.

The waiter returned. She put the book down. The coffee burned her tongue. The flan slipped down her throat like a sweet slug. She read a poem about a quick blue sky and a woman who dreams up a tree. Clare had no idea what the poem meant, but she could not release the image of a woman in a barren field, a tree sprouting up before her. The tree looked real, but was it? If she could climb it, was it real? If she plucked the leaves from the branches, was it real? What was the right test?

Perhaps it was the arguing women who drew her husband's gaze away from the newspaper, allowing the weight of it to rest like a bird on her shoulder. Clare did not move when she felt him looking. Every sound was amplified, but in Havana she could give nothing away. She told herself a killer had injected her with a paralytic drug and now she could not move so much as an inch.

She turned a page, to a line that compared love to a burnt match skating in a urinal. The words merged into a dark mass and hovered before her like a swarm of flies.

Hart Crane was born in Ohio. He committed suicide in the Gulf of Mexico. His father had invented Life Savers candy and how was that for irony.

The waiter nudged along violet-throated pigeons with a broom. She turned to face Richard, using the book to shield the sun from her eyes.

She could see the car hurtling toward him, the hot white ocean of light.

You are dead, she thought. How could you have forgotten?

She had heard of the syndrome that drove people to believe loved ones had been replaced by fakes, but perhaps an inversion existed, one in which the fake was mistaken for the real, and she was afflicted. Yet there was the faint dappling of freckles on his eyelids and the pale comma of a scar above his eyebrow, acquired in a childhood biking accident with his brother, back when they were both blind to their own destinies.

The scar was lighter, and she had to admit there was something slightly different about his nose, or perhaps where his nose stood in relation to his face, as though incredibly subtle plastic surgery had been performed. Such changes might be enough to throw off an acquaintance—who would be relieved to confirm that the man who looked like Richard was in fact not, given that Richard was dead—but she would not be so easily fooled.

On the patio, she sweated heavily under the eyelet dress. *Hello* sounded between her ears, she could feel the word rising up toward her mouth like a balloon into the sky, only to snag on the wet flesh of her throat.

He squinted, as though he was trying to bring her into focus. The delicate whorls of hair on his chest had been lightened by the sun. In their former life, she had started to notice two different versions of her husband dwelling inside the single body. Sometimes she saw the young man, bright and athletic, and then sometimes the older self of the future stepped forward—the whitening hair at his temples, the small hike in the waistline of his jeans. She'd imagined Richard trying to elbow these past and future ghosts away, to make space for the present tense. On the patio, she searched for evidence of the two selves warring inside her husband.

The women had made up and were now leaving the café, arm in arm.

Clare, he said. The sound of her own name coming from his dead mouth made her feel as though her feet had just been severed at the ankles. A flick of his tongue, a sheen on his upper lip. A familiar tick, something he did when he was about to speak and had a difficult piece to say.

She readied herself. A long pause. A canyon.

What, he finally said, are you doing in Havana?

The dreaded question. At long last it was here.

You, she did not tell him. You, you, you. Her tongue stayed still in her mouth. Her arms turned leaden, her fingertips numb: someone had sunk her hands into buckets of ice. She slithered from her chair, and when she was able to look at the world again, she was lying on the patio, the eyelet dress bunched around her thighs, exposing the ugliness of her knees. The waiter was crouched on one side, fanning her with a menu. Her husband was a speck in the corner of her eye. She blinked, her eyelashes laced with sunlight, and two specks appeared in her periphery, her husband and the suited man. She let the waiter help her up. She went straight into the bathroom and vomited, and when she came out, rank and wild-haired, the suited man had returned to his newspaper and Richard was gone.

In this life, that was how their first meeting ended.

In their former life, this was how their first meeting began.

Clare was living in Chicago, working in a university library and trying to understand what she wanted to do with her life. She had been attracted to the geography of Illinois because its landlockedness seemed like the opposite of where she was from, though soon she learned that the shores of Lake Michigan could feel like the brink of an ocean. She had a roommate with a snapping turtle and mold allergies. The toilet was a hysteric, her room subarctic in the winter. Despite these shortcomings the space had felt luxuriantly secluded. At the Seahorse, her mother had tacked a sign that read PRIVATE! to the front door of the attached apartment, and guests still came knocking. Once Clare had been startled to find a couple peering into the living room window; when they saw she was inside, they began to rap frantically on the glass. She had felt like a fish in a bowl.

To be at once loathed and needed—that was the position of the tourist. Clare had often felt needled by the presence of all these strangers, and yet even as a child she understood that the foundation of her life was built on their arrival.

In Florida, she had come to think of her mother's personality as being built of surfaces. Whenever she tried to look more closely, she was blinded by reflections, and when a surface momentarily cracked, the view was often frightening. When Clare was a child, her mother would sometimes slink into her room in the middle of the night and crawl into her bed and weep, their spines pressed together, Clare silent, as though what was occurring was a secret neither of them dared acknowledge— was this what it meant to be an adult woman? In Chicago, she was twenty-five and the ice cube she had pressed against her heart in childhood was proving slow to thaw, and though she longed for such a thawing, the notion also frightened her: she would imagine the pulsing red organ in her chest, warm and exposed. In the meantime, the library was the perfect place to cultivate a second, secret self, with all those hours spent shelving books in silence. She had started to notice people almost exclusively in fragments. An arm under a desk, reaching for a fallen pencil. A back bent over a water fountain. A hand frozen under the amber beam of a lamp.

Away from Florida for the first time, she began to think about the education she had received on being a young woman. How she had been trained to believe that if you risked your body, that most precious commodity, it was only a matter of time before you were punished. No one ever told her this directly, but the instruction was folded into her mother's admonishment to never walk alone at night and the dress code her otherwise lax father suddenly enforced when she went on a date: no shoulders, no belly, nothing short. As though she suddenly did not live in Florida, where the weather demanded skin. As though the presence of skin could drive the boy who was taking her to the movies in the direction of the unspeakable. The way her cut-off shorts and bikini top were blamed when a guest solicited her by the vending machines. He offered her a hundred dollars for five minutes. The slutty girls who died first in horror movies. The girl in her own high school who was raped during prom. The instruction was there in the whispered comments about the dress she had been wearing—the flimsy spaghetti straps, the hem that barely covered her crotch—and how much she'd had to drink.

The rapist had been a student at a different high school, all the way down in Orlando, which seemed to reassure the parents. The danger was always *out there*, humming along the borders of the night. The dangers closest to home were not even discussed in whispers.

In her senior year of high school, she discovered chat rooms, salacious conversations with boys that went deep into the night, and then she began meeting those boys—who sometimes turned out to be men—in shopping center parking lots and in malls and in parks. She lied to her parents, said she was going to a study group or catching a movie with school friends. She never had sex with any of these boys or men. She kissed them. She dry humped. She blew one on a blazing Saturday afternoon, in the far reaches of a Kmart parking lot (back then parking lots were something of a destination). She went skinny-dipping with another, one night in Crescent Beach, and in the water he brushed her wet hair from her face, so very tenderly, and said, I wish I could rape you right now.

Then he laughed and splashed. He was just joking.

The glint of his teeth in the night. Hands like pale fish breaking through the waves. What kind of person do you think I am?

She left these men sweating and frustrated, her own body unscathed. She returned home feeling triumphant. It was not so dangerous out there after all. She had risked her body and she had not been punished.

In Chicago, she looked back on that younger version of herself and felt sick for her.

She'd had no sense of the world, less a mark of innocence than a very particular form of stupidity. She'd had no sense of the terribleness any of those boys or men could have visited upon her, the terribleness for which she would have been utterly unprepared. She almost felt grateful to them for not doing what they could have.

In her junior year of college, in North Florida, her boyfriend picked a fight at a house party and shoved her down a flight of stairs. She could remember the air turning to sludge as his face reddened and contorted into something both unrecognizable and terribly familiar. She would never forget the dumb shock as she watched his hands fly toward her and the way she'd just stood there, frozen as a startled deer. She limped back to her dorm room alone, her bottom lip fat and slick with blood, ribs pulsing. She dumped him immediately and avoided him for the rest of her time on campus—he avoided her just as studiously; perhaps he was ashamed. All that time, the danger had not been *out there*; it had been walking her to class, studying next to her in the coffee shop, sleeping in her bed.

She'd wanted to go home to her parents and ask, *Why didn't anyone tell me?*

In Chicago, Clare liked to use the blood pressure machine at the supermarket. Her blood pressure was normal; she didn't know why she enjoyed the strangling cuff so much, but she found the process meditative. At the machine, she sat so still that a woman once stopped and said she'd nearly mistaken Clare for a mannequin. She would think of that moment again the first time she saw *Killer's Kiss* with Richard, the scene in the mannequin factory where two men fight with axes, hacking naked female mannequins to pieces in the process. She developed ideas about secrecy as armor, an essential privacy. Richard might have fallen into silence in the last year of his life, but certain silences had been embedded in her long ago. So it was not that she'd wanted the second, secret self—it was just that she had never figured out another way to live.

One summer she began to notice a man, tall and honey-haired, following her around campus—or was he? He would trail her for a few blocks and then turn a corner. Had she made him up? One afternoon, though, it was unmistakable: this man *was* following her. He followed her to a nearby coffee shop and lurked by the door and stalked her back toward campus. She remembered sweat between her fingers and toes. The clouds above were a neat grid of white.

When she finally spun around, ready to scream and toss hot coffee in his face if that's what it took to get away, he raised his hands like he was being held up and said, I'm so sorry, I'm acting like a possessed person, I've seen you around the library and I have been wanting to say something to you, to say hello, and I couldn't figure out a way to do it and so now I've gone and done it in the wrongest way possible.

It was his smile, lopsided and shy, that transformed the encounter, turning her nervous and warm and charmed. On the sidewalk, she started to laugh. It was an utterly unexpected moment, the kind that made her life feel a little bit larger.

His irises were a soft chocolate, and soon she would learn that the color could change depending on the light and her vantage. Hazel, goldish.

This has got to be the worst pickup of all time, she said, laughing so hard she had to put her coffee cup down. Like epically, historically bad.

Oh my god, he said, hands dropping to his sides. I know it is. I know.

She was still laughing, almost on her knees with laughter.

It turned out he was in Chicago for a film studies Ph.D. He walked her back to campus. He gave her his number. The rest took care of itself, he would say years later, when telling their story. There were three sides to a marriage: public and private and who-fucking-knows, one lived and one performed and one a thundering mystery. She learned about the performed side because when he told their story he always failed to mention his eventual confession to Clare: that he had felt terribly humiliated by her laughter, even though the way he approached her was plainly ridiculous, even though she had every right to laugh or scream, and he had almost hoped she didn't call and was further humiliated by his elation when she did.

What was it about men and humiliation? Clare had wondered after this admission and would keep wondering as she watched killer after killer respond to humiliation with masks and knives. Was humiliation supposed to be any easier for women to take? She didn't think so, even though the world kept insisting they were built for it.

At two in the afternoon, Clare walked south on a broad avenida in Miramar, past the embassies of France and the Netherlands, mansions with tall gates and green hedges and windswept palms. The ocean was a blue lip to her left, close enough for her to hear the comings and goings of the tide. She had read that, all the way back in the 1900s, little rooms were carved into the walls of the Malecón, so visitors could bathe in the sea and remain cloaked in privacy, a fact that had called to mind the hotels in Florida that had laid claim to portions of public beaches, the particular luxury of being public and private, seen and hidden, at the same time. She passed a slumping hotel with a sun-bleached exterior and tiny, concrete balconies. On one of these balconies, a shirtless man smoked a cigarette, ashing onto the roof of the white Lada idling in the driveway, a yellow taxi sign nestled in the back window. She was in pursuit of the hospital, armed with her

binoculars and her guidebook filled with notations. The structure was yellow and white, with a circular concrete overhang
shading the front steps; tall windows stared out at a Cuban flag
snapping in the breeze. She smelled smoke: a cigarette had
been left burning in the gravel pool of a standing ashtray, the
smoker long gone.

In the soaring lobby, with fluorescent lights glaring down
from the ceiling and hard brown chairs drilled into the floors,
she found intake staffed by a single nurse in scrubs, reading
glasses sitting atop her head like a crown. Clare took out her
phone and scrolled through her photos. Here was Richard sitting across from her at a restaurant. Here was Richard at Grafton Lakes, standing on a rock. Had she seen him?

The nurse was reading a magazine, though perhaps reading
wasn't quite the right word for what she was doing: with a black
marker, she was circling faces, one or two on every page. She
drew the circles studiously. She did not look up at Clare; perhaps her Spanish had not been accurate. Behind them an older
woman with a white streak in her hair was pushing a boy around
in a wheelchair. The boy had a tan patch over his eye, and if the
wheelchair stopped for even a moment, he would unleash a
cataclysmic scream.

Finally the nurse looked at the photo of Richard at Grafton
Lakes. She leaned forward and touched the image, zooming
in. She scratched her temple with the felt tip of the marker,
leaving behind a smudge.

Maybe, she said.

That's good news, Clare said. Do you know where I can find
him?

The nurse shook her head and returned to her circling.

What are you doing with those faces? Clare asked.

The nurse's eyes snapped up. Now she was interested.

I'm making my perfect face, she said. I'm building it from scratch.

When the detectives had asked Clare to describe her marriage, she had said that she and Richard were happy, though the truth was that she did not think of her marriage as having been happy or unhappy—she thought of it as unfinished. They had dated for two years and then married on a lark. This experiment in living had given way to a decade of feet brushing together in bed and bloodied dental floss in the trash and coffee mugs left in the sink and fucking spontaneously at dawn and then not fucking for a month and the pinch pot on the kitchen counter where they abandoned spare change, their joke about how every marriage needed a tip jar. Of following each other up and down stairwells and through parking lots and doorways and shoes crooked in the hallway and damp bath towels on the bedroom floor and hair on pillowcases and food poisoning in the middle of the night and stirring a saucepan on the stove while saying Why Must You Live the Way You Do? or I Would Be Like a Little Boat Cut Loose in a Storm Without You. She knew him as well as she had ever known any other person on earth. She knew all. She knew nothing. Her position depended on the hour or the year or the minute. When he ate green apples, his lips tingled. When distressed, he cleaned with a fervor she found frightening. When things were not going well, and for the last year they had not been going well, all the surfaces were blinding and the condo smelled of bleach; she could even taste the chemicals in their food. The last time she had a fever he lay beside her and dabbed her face with a soaked washcloth, delivering a spectacular cool.

He pointed at the items on restaurant menus when he ordered. Once he noticed a man gawking at her on the street and said, A thing of beauty is to be admired, and she thought but did not say, I'm not a thing, I'm a person. At his college graduation, he lit a cigar as he crossed the stage; having never smoked a cigar before, he vomited in the bushes immediately after. He loved sunrises and Hitchcock and winter walks and licorice candy. She could go on into infinity, and yet she understood that knowing another person was not a stable condition. Knowing was kinetic, ineffable, and it had limits, but the precise location of those limits, the moment at which the knowing stopped and the not-knowing began, was invisible. You would know you had reached the border only after you had surpassed it.

She knew that sometimes her husband talked in his sleep. He would sit up, arms extended. He would stroke one forearm and then another, as though he were washing himself, and say, I'm almost clean, I'm almost clean. Why did she not ever shake his shoulder until he was freed from the landscape of sleep and ask, What is it? What are you talking about? What are you trying to get clean?

Because she had believed in privacy, that most essential armor, and what could be more private than a dream.

Also: she was suspicious of too much honesty, too much openness. She thought couples who claimed to have not a single secret between them sounded deranged. Honesty was trotted out in the name of all kinds of awful things, including cruelty—too much of it could splinter a person.

———

Outside the hospital, she noticed two blue ETECSA public phones bolted into the concrete wall, surrounded by a scattering of flyers. Beneath advertisements for concerts she found a flyer with a photo of a woman in a tweed suit—unsmiling, round glasses, hair in a lacquered bun—who was offering a seminar at the university with a title that Clare understood to mean something along the lines of: quantum physics and the afterlife. The next session was to take place tomorrow afternoon. She took a photo of the address and the time.

At the university, Clare found the woman from the flyer in a windowless classroom, standing at a chalkboard and scratching out a formula. From behind she recognized the tweed skirtsuit, the snug bun. The professor wore stockings, despite the heat, and black pumps. When Clare greeted her in Spanish, she dropped the chalk and whipped around, her palms a ghoulish white. She dusted her hands on her skirt, making a little cloud, and said, in English, I haven't had a student attend this seminar in months. How on earth did you find me?

Clare attempted to explain the flyer. The woman announced herself as Professor Berezniak. She stepped through the cloud of dust, straightened her glasses, and ordered Clare to never speak her terrible Spanish in front of her again; anything less than perfection with respect to the Spanish language was an affront to her ear.

Clare looked at the tornado of equations on the blackboard;

she didn't see how they could make sense to anyone. She asked the professor why she kept holding the seminar if nobody ever comes, and the professor replied that the seminar was a kind of community service, and so while everyone thought she was serving the interests of the community, she was in fact serving the interests of herself.

Former students have found my teaching methods strange and, in some instances, psychologically disturbing, said the professor. Or so I've been told.

I'm already strange, Clare thought, and for all she knew psychologically disturbed too. She had the distinct feeling that Professor Berezniak wished she would conclude this seminar held no interest for her after all and vanish from the afternoon.

Finally the professor sighed and said, Shall we go to my office?

Clare followed her down the hallway to a door so narrow it had to have once belonged to a broom closet. The office was barely large enough for a little round table and two maroon butterfly chairs; it was lit by a lamp with a stained-glass shade. Every inch of wall had been converted into built-in bookshelves. A vintage cuckoo clock announced itself: a miniature door opened, a yellow bird with a red beak pecked the air.

Professor Berezniak said the government had instructed the university to limit air-conditioning use to one hour a day, even in the summer, perhaps in the hope that the heat would root out disloyal academics and sweat them to death.

People tell me I shouldn't talk like this, she continued. But the time has come, I say. The time has come.

Professor Berezniak removed her suit jacket and then her blouse. She did this with great deliberateness, one pearl button at a time, and when she was finished she draped the jacket and blouse over the back of her chair. Underneath she was wearing a white bra with heavy cups and straps. She sat down, flesh crinkling under her rib cage.

I abhor wrinkles, Professor Berezniak said.

Clare sat across from the professor, the library coiling around them.

Well, then? Her tone made it clear that Clare was expected to supply the curriculum. The table between them held a collection of mugs with chipped rims and handles, the bottoms stained black by coffee grounds.

The afterlife, Clare began, then paused. This was not a simple conversation to initiate.

Where is the where? she said next.

The what?

The *where*.

Is that a scientific term?

Tolstoy.

Ah, yes. Tolstoy. Anarchist. Spied on by the Russian secret police. Died in the very same station where he forced poor Anna Karenina in front of that train.

Professor Berezniak spoke of Anna Karenina as though she had been a real person. Her stockings looked ancient; they sagged around her ankles and knees.

A number of years ago there was a study, she said. A study of people who had been blind from birth and who, after near-death experiences, talked about all the things they had been able to *see*. Light, the entirety of the ocean, long-dead ancestors, the history of rocks and insects, their own bodies lying below them, devoid of life.

Clare nodded, expecting her to go on, but she did not.

Well, Clare said. I guess I'm not sure what that proves.

Basic biocentrism! Already the professor was impatient. Perhaps she had not interacted with students in some time.

Look, she continued, all possibilities in the universe are happening simultaneously, but because we, as human beings, are so limited, so very limited, our consciousness collapses all of these possibilities into a single one, which is called our life.

Clare asked if this meant multiple versions of ourselves existed in different places at the same time, imagining a dozen doppelgänger Richards roaming different cities, each indistinguishable from the Richard she had known, the Richard who was no longer alive.

Incorrect! Professor Berezniak said, plucking a tiny ball of lint from her skirt. We have to apply limits on time in order for our brains to make sense of such a concept. Death is one such limit.

Richard had left behind no wishes in the event of his death. At the funeral home, the director had gone over the details of how his body would be prepared for burial: the body would be bathed; his fluids surgically removed; the embalming solution injected into the carotid artery; the body bathed a second time. His service had been held in a church they had never stepped inside, a homily delivered by a priest they had never met—his mother had insisted on this—a priest who told Clare that she should be grateful to God for her pain, because her pain was a sign of her love, and this had left her wanting to spit on the altar.

Months ago, her father had made his wishes clear: cremation, ashes to be scattered in the California town of his birth, far away from Florida.

Pulling a loose thread from the bottom of her skirt, Professor Berezniak went on to say that her mother was Cuban, her father Russian—she herself had spent three years studying physics in Moscow, when she was a young woman. The cold of a Russian winter, she hoped to never feel anything like it again. She had one older brother, who never left Cuba.

He never got to be anything more than a young man, she continued, winding the thread around her finger. He died in Holguín, in 1973. He was killed.

Killed, she repeated.

She added that her parents could have helped her brother, but chose to do nothing, and now that they were dead, she frankly found the unending life of their consciousnesses irritating, she would much rather any trace of them be eradicated altogether, but she couldn't ignore the scientific realities.

My brother on the other hand.

The professor ripped the thread clean from her skirt. A faint halo of red around her mouth, the stubborn remnants of lipstick.

She said, It gives me pleasure to think about his simultaneous possibilities. So let us continue, then, with the simultaneous possibilities.

Let's say you know someone who has changed from one kind of possibility into another, Clare said, selecting her words carefully. Let's just say that such a thing could happen. What do you do then? How do you reach them?

Who says you should do anything at all? Professor Berezniak rubbed her upper lip, erasing the halo. Don't you think it's strange that people believe their current lives, in their current bodies, are the only thing that can contain their consciousness? In a world where we readily consider the possibility of extraterrestrials and déjà vu and reincarnation. In a world where people disappear and never come back.

Clare repeated the word "disappear" and suddenly she was back in her childhood bedroom, curled on her side in the dead of night, her mother's quaking spine pressed to her own. Being this small person and thinking the word "vanish."

Everyone wants to disappear, Professor Berezniak said next.

The two impulses cannot be separated. The desire to have a life and the desire to disappear from it. The world is unlivable and yet we live in it every day. Or do we? We are all erasing ourselves a tiny bit at a time. Drinking, fantasies, secrets, denial, hysteria, double lives, suicide, ennui, schemes. Those are just a few of the ways we disappear.

Clare leaned back in the chair. Sweat ran down her sides. At the Seahorse, her mother had always said that people went on vacations in order to not flee their lives—a temporary abandonment could prevent a permanent one.

Let me raise a single possibility to you, the professor said. Get that little joke? You think you're having some kind of minor existential crisis—I say minor because to have a true existential crisis is a rare thing indeed, and Americans do love to have their little crises in countries that are not their own. You've been spending lots of time drinking in the sun and now you're starting to ask the Big Questions.

My husband died, Clare said. And before that his brother died too.

And my father is not far behind.

And, and, and.

He came from dust and to dust he shall return, the priest had said during the homily.

The professor slipped a finger under her bra strap. The Big Questions ask *us*.

My husband died, Clare said again, louder this time, wanting her voice to shake those books from their shelves. Death could make a person feel righteous in a way they had no right to be. Nothing in the world was less personal and nothing felt more like a poison arrow sent straight for your heart.

Your husband's *body* died. Professor Berezniak coughed, and her bare stomach quivered. She made a motion with her hand that resembled a spider scuttling across a floor.

She said, His consciousness had to go somewhere.

When Clare left the university, it was once again two in the afternoon. At the Third Hotel, she stuffed her backpack until the canvas belly swelled. The last thing she zipped inside was the white box, nested in a coil of T-shirt sleeves, on top of a thin envelope of cash, having finally exchanged the last of her dollars. She left a note on the bedside table in the room because she had a feeling she might not return for some time, and if anyone came looking for evidence of her whereabouts, she did not want to give the impression that she was the kind of woman who went to another country only to go missing or wind up dead.

That afternoon, she did not bother with the hospital. She went straight across the bridge to the aquamarine building with the bountiful yard corralled by green fencing. She passed the gilded mime performing on the Malecón; he stood on an over-turned white bucket, transformed into a statue. A woman in a striped jumper took photos as her child stealthily poked the mime in the side with a miniature Cuban flag. The whole time Clare felt like she was levitating. She kept waiting for someone to point at her feet and say, Look! That woman's levitating! From the sidewalk, it was clear the building was a hostel or a guest house; the familiar blue-and-white placard hung on the chain link. The unoccupied rocking chairs swayed, even though the wind was quiet. A red can of TuKola stood on the edge of the porch. The building was modern but surrounded by ba-roque mansions with vast lots, all in various stages of disrepair. The yellow facade of one house was coated in a gray film, as though someone had carefully painted the exterior with ash. Two were under renovation, caged in scaffolding. A school marked the end of the block, surrounded by a high concrete wall.

She glanced down the sidewalk and caught the eye of a woman in a pink dress and flip-flops, her hair pulled back by a gold clip, a leash connected to a tiny caramel-coated dog looped around her wrist. The woman held Clare's gaze, her mouth sagging into a frown. The dog raised its hind leg to a tree. Clare waved, baring her teeth in a way she hoped looked friendly and noncriminal. The woman turned around and led the dog down the street.

The gate was open, the front door unlocked. Next to the doorbell someone had written out GYM on a strip of duct tape. She picked up the can of TuKola. Empty. The entrance hall was dark. The walls had a damp, sweet smell. Huge elephant-ear plants in chipped clay pots loomed like alien life forms, their green leaves, wide as faces, brushing the ceiling.

On the ground floor, only one room faced the alleyway. The door was locked.

Every September of Clare's childhood, her mother packed a bag and drove away for the month. She never said where she was going and the details of her trips were never discussed when she returned. Once she drove all the way out to California. Once she drove to Mexico City. She called every Sunday, around dinnertime. She sent exactly one postcard. From Point Reyes. The Grand Canyon. Acapulco. Once, while her mother was gone, her father accidentally locked himself out of the business office and then showed his daughter how to get inside.

Clare unzipped her backpack and dug out her wallet, for her credit cards were suddenly not so useless after all. She slid a card into the crack between the door and the jamb. She bent the card toward the knob and away; the lock popped open.

His room had the texture of a crime scene. Everywhere she saw slight disorder. The bed was unmade. Pants had been tossed on the floor, the cloth legs splayed. The lamp shade was crooked, the inside spotted with amber burns. The single chair was pulled away from the table, as though the occupant had gotten up abruptly. The window blinds were half-raised and hanging in a tilt. A rotary phone sat on the bedside table, the cord a tangle. The wallpaper had bubbled from the humidity.

She investigated the bathroom and found an empty medicine cabinet with rusted hinges. A pair of damp red socks had been slung over the shower rod, left to dry. She rushed back into the bedroom when she heard the sound of a cat crying. She stopped in front of the ceramic black-and-white cat and felt a surge of relief when she realized it was animated, programmed to blink and flick its tail and release a robotic meow. She picked up the cat and shook it. Meow, meow, the animal wailed. She felt like she was levitating again. She put the cat down. All the surfaces wobbled.

A wall closet with wicker slats faced the bed. She opened the doors, pushed aside three pairs of identical slacks, found nothing else. The closet wasn't quite tall enough for her to stand inside, so she sat on the floor, hugged her knees to her chest. Through the slats she watched daylight sculpt shadows on the wood floor.

She pressed a hand against the wall. Her skin was slick, and she imagined Richard finding sweat marks in the shape of palms, the work of an overheated ghost.

A hard ball of pressure collected in her stomach. She heard a door slam. Clacking footsteps in the room above, as though someone were stomping around in wood clogs. Water rushing through the pipes hidden behind the walls. Every sound made her heart jackknife in her chest.

One September, when Clare was twelve, a Cat 3 hurricane barreled into Jacksonville Beach. Her mother was in Maine for the month. The guests at the Seahorse were evacuated, but Clare and her father stayed. She remembered watching families pack their cars, windswept, eyes flitting up toward the cloud-clotted sky. She remembered wondering if she and her father would have to hide in a closet or under a bed. On the way to the community center to collect sand bags, he told her they would not be alone that night; as it happened, one guest had stayed behind and they would be taking her in.

When they returned, a woman was standing by the attached apartment. She was thin and fair, dressed in jeans and a black leotard top. She was barefoot, a detail that had startled Clare with its casualness, even though people went barefoot in Florida all the time. Her chestnut hair was in a ponytail, tied with a red kerchief, showing off a smooth forehead and shell-shaped cheekbones. Her name was Ellis Martin.

In the apartment, her father went to work boarding up windows. Clare sensed it was her job to entertain this stranger now standing in their living room.

My car broke down, Ellis Martin said, retying her kerchief. Her top had a scooped back, a black satin bra strap pressed tight against her spine, the hooks pulling. Her shoulders were freckled. When she moved, Clare could make out the knots of vertebrae sliding around under her skin.

My mother's car broke down once, Clare said. In Saratoga Springs. She called Triple A and they took care of everything.

Well, Ellis Martin said, I don't have Triple A.

How are you enjoying Florida? Clare was repeating a line she'd overheard her mother say to guests. In their presence, she would turn outward, like a flower finally afforded the right degree of sun.

The weather could be better, Ellis Martin said, curling her toes. She pulled out a pack of cigarettes and lit one right in the living room. She blew smoke toward the ceiling and told Clare not to worry. She was a doctor and she knew the risks.

Clare offered Ellis Martin, who had tiny feet, the spare pair of jelly sandals by the door. Maybe this woman really was in some kind of desperate situation, to have shown up at the apartment without any shoes. Ellis Martin gave the jellies a long, disdainful look and told Clare that the sandal was a grotesque invention. They flayed and pinched and squeezed—few things were less flattering. She preferred her feet to be completely covered or bare.

Clare wondered if Ellis Martin was aware that she was in Florida, where no one spoke ill of the sandal, though much later she would learn this woman lived several hundred miles south, in Port St. Lucie. Perhaps, at the time of this first meeting, her address had been elsewhere. When Clare thought back on that night, she could remember the sound of her father hammering, the attached apartment growing darker one window at a time, casting shadows across the face of Ellis Martin as she exhaled— and, she could only assume, her own. It had felt like sitting inside a mouth that was slowly closing.

It was evening when Richard returned to the room, carrying a brown paper sack. She pressed her fingers between the slats, her eyes into the narrow opening. She was hunched between two pant legs, a swath of fabric hanging on either side of her face like blinders. He did not seem hesitant or suspicious; she had concealed her presence well.

The rotary phone sounded. He placed the sack on the unmade bed and answered, the receiver pressed tight to his ear. He tapped his index finger on the bedside table. He was silent and yet a conversation, an exchange of some kind, was ongoing; she could tell by the density of the air. She considered the possibility that through some freak mishap in the laws of physics, he had been vaulted into *a* future, a future where he lived and boarded the flight to Havana, but at the same time it was not quite *his* future; he was someone else here. Could this have been what Professor Berezniak had been suggesting? She felt like she needed to spend a year reading about physics and philosophy and then visit the professor again.

The moment he hung up, he kneeled and pulled a black duffel bag out from under the bed. Clare recoiled into the shadows, certain that he was going for the closet, that any minute he would hurl open the door and there would be nothing left for her to do but scream and leap out, like the killer she had decided to be. Instead he emptied the paper sack into the duffel. A dozen mangoes spilled out, all gleaming green. He added the red socks hanging in the bathroom, a bar of soap. He appeared to be packing for a trip.

When he left again, his luggage still on the bed, lavender clouds had thickened the sky and the room was shadowed. She slipped out of the closet and switched on the lamp, lighting up the crooked shade. The room felt smaller than it had before. A train ticket now sat on the bedside table, pinned under the base of the lamp. In her guidebook, she wrote down the departure time and the destination: tomorrow morning, Cienfuegos. She consulted the map in her guidebook; the city was about a hundred and fifty miles from Havana, on the southern coast. The rotary phone started up again, the ringing so forceful the table shuddered on its stubby legs.

She heard a noise outside and looked out just in time to see a man in a dark suit skirting the side of the building. She rushed to the window and shoved away the blinds. The alley was unlit, the shadows too dense to see clearly, but she could have sworn she glimpsed this man scurrying up a tree. The rotary phone was still ringing and the noise was having a physical effect on Clare; it was as though she had swallowed the bell and now it was sounding inside her body, shaking her organs from their cavities.

She picked up. The line was riddled with static.

Hello, she said in Spanish, holding the phone away from her ear.

She could make out a voice, but the crackle made it hard to discern much more. She hunched over, hollowing out her stomach. She imagined vanishing into the line and bursting into whatever space the voice was originating from.

She said hello once more. For a moment, the line cleared. A voice said hello back.

She dropped the phone. The handset bounced in the receiver and then went still.

The entrance door slammed open and shut. The bubbled walls trembled. She turned the lamp off and rushed back into the closet. Once in the room, Richard went straight into the bathroom. He left the door cracked open, the light bleaching a patch of floor. She listened to the toilet flush, the faucet run, the water shooting around behind the walls. All those worlds within worlds making themselves known.

In the bedroom, he pushed aside the black duffel bag and lay flat on the mattress, eyes closed, palms folded on his stomach. He had left the bathroom light on, so the room was half-lit. All through the night she watched him lying there. His mouth was soft, his eyelids still, his breathing even. He really did seem to be asleep.

Scopophilia, or the morbid urge to gaze.

The word had appeared numerous times in one of Richard's papers; at their kitchen table, she had found it difficult to pronounce. Horror films were designed to assault the eye, he'd written. They satisfied the audience's secret desire: to stare into the abyss and confront whatever existed there and then be ushered safely back to the familiar, the very process that Arlo found so objectionable. She had not thought about that word for a long time, but in the closet it returned to her. Through the years she had learned a lot from her husband.

At dawn, the phone rang and he jerked awake. He rolled away and squeezed a pillow over his head. Clare sat coiled behind the pant legs. Her spine was a hot curve of pain, her mouth as dry as a stone.

The caller had been a woman, and Clare had to admit, if only to herself, that the voice had sounded very much like her own.

During her final trips to Nebraska, Clare skipped business dinners and spent the evenings driving silent country roads, earning reprimands from her boss. She did not want to go back to her room and listen to the rattle of the ice machine. She wanted to keep going—but not to a place she had been before. She turned off the headlights. The darkness sudden and complete. The pressure of her shoe on the gas. The weight of her hands on the wheel. She felt immortal. She turned the headlights back on and drove for a little while and then switched them off again. Five seconds. Ten. In New Scotland, she would not tell Richard, would shield him from the inner ugliness only she could see: the part of her willing to drive in blindness even if it introduced the possibility of running over a dog or a human being. Consider how the initial confession of the dark headlights would lead to more questions and where those questions would lead—Why did you miss these dinners? Did you not care about being fired? Why were you acting reckless and insane?

Maybe the person who struck and killed her husband had been driving with their headlights off too; maybe they had not been drunk or homicidal; maybe they had just been trying to shock themselves out of their own skin. Maybe her own negligence and her husband's death were connected in this way. After he was killed, she turned on her headlights at the earliest threat of rain or evening, but it was too late.

It could have been me.

At first, she tried to keep this thought hidden, but in time she began to welcome the thought, because if she was somehow culpable, if she was party to the crime, then there existed a direct and useful set of actions for her to undertake. She could admit, she could atone, she could solve. She could claim her unforgivable act and assure herself that she would never again commit another.

In the morning, the train lurched from the La Coubre station with a shriek and a hot gust of smoke. When Richard saw her at the opposite end of the car, he fled down the aisle and through a rusted vestibule door. She followed him into the next car and the next. He was light on his feet, swift in the face of the doors. She kept grasping the worn seatbacks for support and heaving herself against the heavy doors, yanking them open in time to see his figure pause at the top of the car before disappearing.

The train was crowded, the overhead racks bursting with luggage and plastic shopping bags, the bottoms stretched and bulging. She passed a family of three, the parents bouncing a little boy in red shorts on their knees, singing a song. A woman wrote furiously in a spiral notebook, her hair a lick of brown between her shoulder blades. A man in a Mets cap slept against a giant duffel bag, his wrists crossed over the top. Two teenage girls sat close together, sharing the black headphones attached to a Walkman.

Finally Richard was out of cars, at the top of the train, cornered. There was no place left for him to go unless he planned to work his way back to the other end or fling himself onto the tracks. She did not want to encourage such rash behavior; she would have to be very careful. She imagined the zookeepers slowly circling the loose ostrich on a street in Havana, armed with a tranquilizer dart and a very large net.

When he sat down, she slipped into a seat five rows back.

She felt the train gain speed, though she could not be sure if that was happening only in her imagination.

Clare understood the mystery at hand to be not a new mystery, but a continuation of the one that had presented itself in New Scotland. She was being granted a chance to follow that story through to its end, and she understood it was a very rare thing, to get that kind of chance. She believed that if she and Richard kept following their private plans together, in parallel, these separate plans might align, merge into one.

She watched the sway of Richard's honeyed head. The window was smudged by the ghost outlines of palms and her own reflection, caught in the glass. The train they were riding was called the French Train, and it had gotten its name, she had read, because the trains had been purchased secondhand from French railways.

They passed green fields bordered by round hills, scattered with grazing goats. She watched a piebald goat stretch its neck, claim the green crown of a branch. Through her binoculars she could make out cement houses tucked into hillsides. A restaurant sign painted in blue on the round end of a gas tank. A swath of red earth slicing a path through the grass. She was surprised by the vastness of the countryside; without her binoculars those hillsides looked to be a lifetime away.

She tore out a piece of paper from the back of her guidebook and found a pen in her backpack. STOP RUNNING AWAY FROM ME! WHERE ARE YOU EVEN GOING? She crept to the front of the car and dropped the note by Richard's feet. He looked straight ahead, his hands folded in his lap. He did not acknowledge her. From her seat she watched him pick up the paper, and as they passed flat fields, restless with cows, he returned the paper to her in the exact same manner. She snatched up the note and was able to understand, through patterns of scrunched letters that transformed into words, into the communication of meaning, from the dead to the living, that he had written the name of a hotel, along with a room number and a time. She held the paper close to her face.

The sloping, cursive script did not quite look like his former handwriting and somehow did not quite *not* look like it either.

The hotel name was familiar, one she could place in the Escambray Mountains. At one of the festival receptions, she had overheard a couple talking about their recent stay in the hotel. Under Batista, the property had been used as a tuberculosis sanatorium, and now it was a hotel that catered to health tourists and ecotourists; for a fraction of a second she was overcome by the worry that she was following a common medical tourist into the mountains. The most enthusiastic ecotourist she'd ever known drank his coffee from Styrofoam cups. This hotel sat in the middle of a subtropical forest. The couple from the reception had extolled the virtues of the hydromassage and the birding. The way they had pronounced the name made it sound like "Cure Hotel."

Across the aisle a man pulled a cigarette from a wrinkled

red-and-white package. He stared at the end of the cigarette before lighting it. Next to him sat a young woman in peculiar clothes: a straw hat, a checkered dress with a large bow at the waist, hiking boots with wool socks. How was she not on fire? She was reading *War and Peace* in Spanish, the spine bolstered by duct tape. Clare wondered if she had gotten to the part about the bear.

Clare spotted a truck parked at the mouth of a dirt road, a sticker that translated into TRANSPORTATION OF THE FUTURE pasted across the tailgate. The fields were taking on a wild verdancy. The train passed horses chest-high in grass, the green tips bowed by wind. She felt a warm drip on her knee. She looked up. The roof of the French Train was leaking, even though it had not rained in several days.

An hour later, the train stalled on the tracks. A little girl in a purple dress ran up and down the aisles, smacking the backs of seats. The sun burned through the windows. Clare tried to remain fixed on her husband's figure five rows ahead, tried to be a good detective, but there was the stillness and the sun and the lack of sleep stalking her like a wolf, and soon she was slipping down into the warm stickiness of her seat.

When she woke they were moving again. She looked out in time to catch the concrete slab of an uncovered platform and the hunched old man standing there, brandishing a black umbrella at the passing train.

The swell and burn of her bladder drove her from her seat, in search of a bathroom, found three cars down, tight as a coffin with a jagged hole in the floor; through it she could see bits of passing land: snatches of green, gray streaks of gravel, the thick iron veins of the tracks. No mirror. She was relieved to not confront her reflection. No sink, no lock on the door, no toilet paper. She went quickly, a hot stream in the bowl.

On her way back to her seat, she noticed a man in a suit sitting alone, body coiled against the window. He did not notice her—he was engrossed in reading an orange guidebook titled *The Pocket Atlas of Remote Islands*—but she recognized him as the man from the café in Miramar. The man with the flaxseed mustache and her father's forehead. On the French Train, he looked perturbed: frowning as he turned the pages, his dark, padded shoulders pressed to his ears, his brow scrunched. Clare hurried back to her seat, a funny feeling zapping around in her stomach.

Horror films had taught her that a person could will a thing into existence, but once it was outside their consciousness, the consciousness that had been busily inventing simultaneous possibilities, it became a force unto itself, ferocious and uncontrollable. Maybe some invisible corner of her consciousness had willed her husband's return, but surely that corner had not intended to also conjure a duffel bag filled with mangoes or a man who ran away from her or a rotary phone that wouldn't stop ringing. The character then had to do battle with the part of themselves responsible for the conjuring, in addition to battling the consequences of the conjuring itself. For example, if she had conjured the victim of a crime, it stood to reason that she might also have conjured the killer—not *the* killer, perhaps, but *a* killer, a person they were now meant to flee.

Clare sat inside a very long silence, though it was not really a silence at all: she could hear the train clacking over the tracks, pages turning, breaths, coughs, squeaking seats, an old man farting, children arguing in Spanish, matches struck, cigarettes lit, the near imperceptible gust of time passing, wind. She had crumpled up the note and left it on her seat, which now seemed very foolish, in the event that they were being followed.

She stared at the back of Richard's head so hard he blurred and multiplied, like he was being replicated right in front of her, and then she ate the paper.

The train stopped again. Through the window she saw a dark green lagoon, bordered by marshland, clouds reflected in the water. One row ahead someone had placed a white paper cup upside down on the floor, so it looked like a little castle. On the French Train, you could buy coffee, but you were expected to provide your own cup. Her skin was pink and tender and warm. She felt raw with alertness and exhaustion. She imagined the paper dissolving in her stomach. The ink. She felt empty and full. She yawned against her will, her mouth prying itself open. Other passengers were falling asleep (heads tipped against windows, foreheads poised on the backs of seats), as though a spell of somnolence had been cast over the car. Even Richard was slumping over, five rows ahead. Clare drifted off once more, and when she woke, he had vanished from his seat and the train was pulling into Cienfuegos.

When Clare arrived at the Albany precinct, her husband had been dead for forty-eight hours. At night, she would imagine the person who killed him driving on; she would will their car to spontaneously combust. She had been sleeping with the sealed white box on the bedside table, and she could not help but think that it was the ideal size for a human ear.

The police station had been cold. Inside she had wanted to keep her coat and gloves and hat on, but it felt strange to do so once seated across from the detectives, both in short sleeves, adapted to the temperature. She did not want to appear in a hurry; it was hard to imagine what she would be hurrying for now. She took off her hat. She kept her gloves and coat on, the zipper pulled to her chin.

At the precinct, she learned there were no traffic cameras on that stretch of road. It had been dark out, and they had not succeeded in securing an eyewitness. They were still awaiting the forensics—tire marks, debris—and the autopsy report. In the meantime, the only other available evidence was the Good Samaritan's account of the scene and her own account, of her husband.

They asked if she was ready to begin.

They wanted to know where she was at the time of the hit-and-run. She had been on a conference call; she provided the relevant names and information.

Just so we can get that out of the way, Detective Winter said.

They asked if he had been acting like himself, if she had noticed anything unusual.

Silently she began a list. He was newly skittish around dogs and he had stopped eating bananas and he walked like he was in a dream and he had a notebook filled with ideas about zombies, presumably in preparation to see Yuniel Mata's film. From this notebook, she'd learned that William Seabrook had boasted about being the first to colonize *zombi* into "zombie" after a trip to Haiti—made possible by the American occupation, which spanned from 1915 to 1934, nearly twenty years. Apparently William Seabrook had also been a renowned sexual sadist. She read a quote attributed to Zora Neale Hurston: "He can never speak again, unless he is given salt." She learned that in 1887 Lafcadio Hearn was hired to write about the French West Indies. In Martinique, after hearing the word *zombi* for the first time, he went looking for a definition. He was told that if he is walking the road late at night and sees a great fire and the closer he gets to the fire the more it moves away—that is the work of the *zombi*. He was told that a *zombi* is a horse with three legs and a nightmare in which a familiar person transforms into unspeakable evil.

A white box, the edges taped shut, and she had no idea what was inside.

She did not know what any of this added up to.

What qualifies as unusual? she said.

Anything that comes to mind, Detective Winter said. Anything at all.

He seemed preoccupied, she began.

For how long? the detectives wanted to know.

A while. She paused. Close to a year.

That's a long time to be preoccupied, Detective Hall said.

More questions followed. Did he have trouble at work, did he have enemies, a history of mental illness, debt, bad habits, had he deviated from his usual routines. She felt like she was standing in another room, listening to the conversation through a wall.

She removed her right glove.

He took walks every evening, she said. That was a normal part of his routine.

The side of Route 443 doesn't seem like a very restful place for leisure walking.

Detective Winter was right. All this time she had imagined her husband walking the quiet streets in their neighborhood, or over to Elm Avenue Park. She tried to picture that stretch of Delaware Avenue—what was there? A bagel place with suicide lighting, a car wash, a knitting shop. She imagined her husband sitting alone in a booth and eating a bagel, his tongue thick with cream cheese. She imagined cars whipping past him on the road, the fright of one coming too close.

He was writing a book, she said.

And was that unusual?

No. He had published widely in his field.

This was both true and not: he had published a great many papers, but he had never before finished a book. She understood the manuscript to be half-completed at the time of his death, and right then a few lines from it appeared in the air—*Both city and zombie have a talent for transformation. The surface of a city transmutes as a person moves across it and then covers their tracks—and because we loathe the eradication of our presence, we make new movements. To live in a city is to be engaged in an endless cycle of self-erasure and self-assertion, ignorant of the zombie worlds, with their own restless cycles of transformation, plotting to proclaim their own existence.*

Her hands looked so strange now, one gloved and one not.

And what was the title of this book? asked Detective Winter. It was called *The Nightmare Is Near*.

The detectives appeared interested and confused. She tried her best to explain about the Terrible Place, how it was meant to embody the worst capacities of the human soul, how it could sometimes be a small space, like a tunnel or a basement, or it could be an entire city like Washington, D.C., or Barcelona or Paris or Havana.

And was this a new . . . interest? Detective Winter asked.

She waved her gloved hand. Horror films were his area of study, she said. His specialty. I'm sorry. I should have mentioned that before.

Detective Hall wanted to know what she did for a living. Clare relayed the particulars of her job.

You must hear a lot of jokes, Detective Winter said. About elevators.

Not really, said Clare.

Elevator jokes are a genre, Detective Winter said. Like, two people are on an elevator. One asks the other how their day's going and that person says, Oh, you know, filled with ups and downs.

Clare stared at the detectives.

So you spend a lot of time on the road? said Detective Hall.

Yes. Clare removed her left glove. Yes, I do.

Recently, on a flight to Columbus, she had sat next to a passenger who wrote for a newspaper. He had started in the obituaries and worked his way up, though he noted that any reporter in the building could write an obituary if called upon, just as any good solider could be a foot solider if there was a need.

Richard's obituary had appeared in the Albany *Times Union*. His brother's had appeared in *The San Diego Union-Tribune*. Her father's would appear in *The Florida Times-Union*.

The man went on to say that the paper was in a small town, and the thing that had surprised him the most was the volume of obituaries: around five a day, forty a week. He had not realized that, in this little town, so many people were dying. On the rare occasion that there were no deaths to report, the newspaper had to run a statement to that effect. Otherwise people would call, demanding to know what had happened to the obituaries.

All that time away must make it hard to know what's really going on at home, Detective Hall said. She wore a wedding ring with a cloudy stone, and Clare detected an edge of accusation in her voice.

Did you have a nice wedding? Detective Winter asked.

The question struck Clare as peculiar and unnecessary, but she did not want to appear uncooperative.

Our wedding was a long time ago, Clare said, though as it happened their wedding *had* been nice, a courthouse ceremony in San Diego followed by a small gathering of family and friends at Sunset Cliffs Park, picnic baskets packed with strawberries and tea sandwiches. Cheap, sweet champagne. The lightness of the lark, the high-hearted plunge into the unknowable.

You're right, Detective Hall said. Your wedding was a long time ago. Ten years by our count. Yet in my own experience I

LAURA VAN DEN BERG

have found it useful to look back on the point of origin, especially when I'm in need of a reminder as to why I wanted to get married at all.

I know why I wanted to get married, Clare said. I don't need a reminder.

She had never been drawn to ritual. She had only attended religious services for weddings and funerals. She had skipped her own graduations. Yet she'd permitted herself to imagine that the particular leap of marriage might bring about a sense of completeness, would perhaps even provide an answer to an invisible question, one that she could sense, could almost taste in the back of her mouth, but could not articulate.

Of course, marriage had not led her to a sense of completeness. Rather, it introduced different sets of questions, one after another, and ultimately led her to the drastic incompleteness of being married to a man whose death, the exact circumstances, was uncertain. If a death was uncertain, a life in turn was made uncertain—or the uncertainty that had always been there was exposed. In hindsight, it seemed like a near-radical act on their part to not have children, to refuse that natural narrative impulse for closure. Closure in the sense that the purpose of your marriage was inarguable—to produce this child—and that a person's essence still claimed a place in the world; in this way the dead could continue to move forward in time.

No one would think her father's death was uncertain, Clare thought in the interrogation room. Everyone would assume they knew the cause.

She unzipped her coat. She focused on the sound of the teeth separating. She had not done a very good job of explaining their life.

Clare, Detective Winter said, is there something you want to tell us?

She closed her eyes. She wanted to tell these detectives the single truest thing she knew. If she could only sink below the current surface of her thoughts. She felt a few degrees away from that place, and yet at the moment the distance was unbridgeable.

I just— she started, then realized she had no idea where she meant to go, no verbal path to follow.

She opened her eyes.

I just— she tried again, but stopped when she noticed the detectives making eye contact. On Detective Hall, she thought she saw the slightest hint of a smile.

I'm sorry, Detective Winter said. It's a bit of a running joke between us, as partners. When people start a sentence that way.

I just, I just, Detective Hall said, a false pitch creeping into her voice. Was Clare being mocked?

Detective Winter closed the folder. It is, in our opinion, the worst way to start a sentence in the English language.

Later she would wonder if the detectives had suspected she was the one who hit her husband with the car and fled the scene, if they had checked her alibi the moment she left the station, expecting to find a gap in her story. When she spoke next with the colleagues who had been on the conference call, she had searched for the scent of mistrust in the air.

The mountain air was cool and thin. From the train station, it had taken an hour by taxi to reach the Cure Hotel, the fee nearly flattening Clare's envelope of cash. The white Lada had labored going up the steep road, stuttering so badly the driver had to drop her a mile south of the hotel. Now she stood light-headed, her thighs quivering, in front of a concrete hulk surrounded by mountain forest, a hundred block-shaped windows peering out on a vast green lawn. The structure was ten stories high and looked like a Soviet relic, a concrete space station abandoned to nature, except it was not abandoned at all. People in matching beige tracksuits—guests, she assumed—were milling around the grounds, stomping on the light fog rising from the grass like smoke.

In the lobby, the ceiling was flat and low, the tile floor and furniture the same shade of beige as the tracksuits. An impressive amount of art hung on the walls—large, colorful abstract paintings in black frames. The reception desk was surrounded by tall ferns. They looked a lot like the ferns her mother had kept in the lobby of the Seahorse.

A man in a red polo shirt checked her in. She asked him for the room number her husband had written down; indeed there was a vacancy. Behind him an open door looked down a short hallway and into an office, where a woman sat at a boxy desktop. She wore a green blouse, the arms printed with turquoise butterflies. She had perfect posture, but her carriage struck Clare as artificial, the kind of person who was always imploring herself to *sit up*. Clare wondered if she was writing a memo or a manual or a death threat.

The people in identical beige tracksuits continued to stream in and out of the lobby. When Clare asked about them, the man said there were two kinds of people staying here: patients and guests. If she wanted to become a patient, she could do so at any time, provided she was able to pay the fees. He said the hotel specialized in the relief of pain. Their approach was to consider the entire patient: a backache was not simply a backache, but a symptom of something greater; if they found the root of the problem together, the pain could be eliminated.

This man had the starched, upright manner of a person working hard to contain a well of deep feeling. Even the collar of his red polo had been carefully pressed. She could imagine how all these people showing up with their suitcases full of pain would take its toll.

He handed her a brochure for their hydromassage chamber.

Clare thanked him for the information and fled.

She walked quickly down a long, cold hallway, her footsteps echoing.

She had an hour to kill, according to the paper her body was presently digesting, and so she followed signs for the hotel restaurant, which led her down one corridor and then another, each a little darker, a little chillier, than the one before. At the restaurant, she was the only guest, though judging by the track-suits there were plenty of patients. She sat in a rattan chair and swallowed a glass of lukewarm water in two gulps. She ordered a pan con queso, all the while assuring herself that she was not, in fact, traveling alone.

She unzipped her backpack and placed the white box on the table. Oil from her fingers had left translucent circles on the outside; the top was dented, the tape loosening at the edges. The box seemed less troublesome somehow out here in the mountains.

She stared down at the box. She poked it with a spoon. She did not hear any kind of movement inside, and for a moment she imagined raising the lid and finding nothing but air.

She brought the box close to her face. She loosened the tape on one side and pushed the lid up a little. She peered into the tiny slit, her eyelashes scratching the cardboard.

A reel of film, small enough to fit in the palm of her hand. She put the box down.

The air-conditioning was so forceful that she was shivering in her chair, a cloth napkin spread across her knees for warmth. No one in the restaurant was taking photos.

Her food arrived and she devoured half her sandwich. She stuffed the box back into her backpack and left in search of the bathroom; it had been hours since the train. When she returned, the sight of her own half-eaten meal stopped her. Before she had been sitting with her back to the entrance, but her plate and water glass had been moved to the opposite side of the table, as though she had been facing the doorway. Her napkin had been sitting to the left of her plate. Now it rested against the translucent belly of the glass. A waiter with a tray wove around the tables; the patients in beige tracksuits lifted forks. On some tables, red roses stood in slim silver vases, the edges blackened, as though someone had been burning them. She pinched a leaf and made contact with stiff plastic. A ceiling fan turned slowly above. She was still very hungry, so she sat within this new configuration and finished her lunch, even though it looked as though a different person had been eating at this table, filling her with the fear that she was somehow consuming what did not belong to her.

The elevator was out of service. She climbed a hulking stone staircase to a monochrome hallway, the walls and carpeting that now-familiar beige. There she was troubled to discover sounds emanating from the room they were supposed to be checking into. She pressed her ear to the door, catching hushed voices and a light thumping, as though someone was slapping the bedspread. She heard a scream and leapt back, into the center of the hall. The room key was old-fashioned, a brass stone in her hand. She squeezed the serrated teeth.

She kneeled on the carpet and peered through the bell-shaped keyhole. She imagined her iris telescoping into the room and reporting back on what was going on in there, and this visualization exercise was something of a success because she was able to make out a man and a woman fucking on a bed. She could hear the hungry panting. She could see the jerking limbs, the quivering flesh. Her vantage had severed their heads from their bodies. Their feet waved back and forth like hands. Their knees were blurred orbs.

What are you doing? a familiar voice said.

She was startled to look up and see Richard standing over her. He set his duffel bag down on the carpet. He held the same heavy, toothed key, and he was insisting their room was in fact across the hall from the one she had just been spying on. He had snuck up on her, as she'd not thought to check to make sure she wasn't being followed.

We're in room number seven, she whispered, not wanting to disturb the headless couple.

Yes, number seven. He pointed at the opposite door.

His eyes were bright, his hands clean. His pants looked like they had just been ironed. How had his arrival been so effortless? She supposed the dead played by a different set of rules.

She shook her head, mouth sealed tight. He shrugged and unlocked the door.

She stood, knees inflamed from the carpet.

See? he said, stepping grandly into the empty room.

The room overlooked a terrace that bled into an emerald expanse of forest, iced with fog. A man was sitting down there, reading a book. Clare was watching from too great a distance to see the book—to see if it was, as she suspected, *The Pocket Atlas of Remote Islands*—or even the man himself, but he radiated familiarity, and it was not the comforting kind. Dread fell like a mist. She got her binoculars, but by the time she returned to the window the man was gone. She felt even more uneasy with him no longer in sight. Now he could be anywhere: outside their door, in the stairwell, hiding in the shower with a knife.

When she turned from the window, her husband was leaning against a wall, his black duffel at rest by his feet. He had stepped out of his shoes, kept his socks, the red ones she had seen hooked over the shower rod.

Well, Richard said. I guess we're finally going to have that talk.

She told herself she was not unwilling.

She sat down on the edge of the hard bed. She felt like she was back in the police station, unsure of to what extent to disrobe, the implications of doing too little or too much. She kept her shoes on. The furnishings were simple, a mountaintop dormitory. The room was curiously scentless. A sheet with a welcome message, sealed inside a plastic sleeve, lay on the rectangular dresser. The message, in English and in Spanish, read WELCOME AND GOOD LUCK!

Are you planning on getting into a tracksuit? Clare said. She wondered if his body temperature seemed lower by about, say, five degrees. The corn-silk hair at his temples was even lighter, almost luminescent, and his expression still suggested he was thinking deeply about a problem he could not share.

I'm beyond the reach of their methods, he said. You might be too.

Clare remembered what the man in the red polo, the man who looked like he knew plenty about pain, had said about finding the root of the problem; he had made it sound as straightforward as digging around in the dirt and pulling a plant out by the tendrils.

What are you doing here? she said. Where are you going?

I'm in terrible trouble, Richard said. I'm being pursued.

Pursued by who? The fat vein pulsed around her anklebone.

His tongue flicked across his lips. His eyes narrowed.

By you, I had assumed.

By *me*? Your own wife?

You have to admit you've been acting rather strangely.

You're the one who's been acting strangely!

Like the great change had continued even after his death.

Strange is a sliding scale, I suppose. He bent a knee, pressed a socked foot flat against the wall. A phone rang in the room

144

next door. He explained that he was being followed, that he had been receiving threatening phone calls, and when he saw her in Havana—well, he drew the logical conclusion.

I can help, Clare said. I'm becoming an expert in surveillance.

He crossed his arms and tipped his head against the wall, dubious. What would you know about surveillance?

This time, she would not be a sight. She would create one.

Clare picked up a chair and jammed the back under the doorknob, barricading them inside. As she rooted around in her backpack for her nail scissors, she counted the rules for hiding. Don't go into attics or basements; avoid the dark; forget all about showers; lock yourself in the closet; jam the chair under the door; be willing to adopt a disguise; never, under any circumstances, investigate a curious sound.

Case in point: right now she was hearing what sounded like a wailing through the walls. Would she knock on that person's door and see if they were all right? Certainly not.

In this way, at least, they were prepared.

In the bathroom, she unbuttoned his shirt, one pearl circle at a time. She thought about Professor Berezniak and her abhorrence of wrinkles. She patted down the soft hair on his sternum. She felt around inside his belly button. She slid off his shirt, right arm and then left, and hung it on a hook. She turned him around. She inspected the mole on his lower back, the scent of his armpits. She raised a hand and examined his oval fingernails; they were impossibly clean.

She could not find any bruising or lacerations or scars. No evidence at all of his accident, if "accident" was indeed the right word.

Richard sat on the toilet seat and she trimmed his hair until it was shorn close to the scalp. The bathroom was free of windows. The walls had been painted a nauseating green. It felt to her like a covert space.

Careful, he kept telling her as she cut. Careful.

Height brought clarity. That had been one of her father's sayings. From the top of a skyscraper you could see the shape of a city. From the peak of a mountain, the surrounding land. He had grown up in the Sierra Nevadas and had never liked the flatness of Florida. He felt the absence of elevation interfered with perspective.

She rubbed a hand over Richard's head and felt a satisfying prickle.

He stood and surveyed the fallen hair around his feet, his face flushed and crumpled. He batted at his shoulders with a towel. She peeled off her shirt. Her bra smelled of sweat and sadness. Blood moved at top speed through the tunnels in her body. She handed him the scissors and asked him to make her look less like herself.

On the toilet, she tried to concentrate on how solid the floor felt under her feet, how cold and hard. She pushed the loose molar. She felt Richard begin to gently collect fistfuls of her brown hair. It was the plainest shade imaginable: not red enough to be auburn, not light enough to be dishwater blond. She did not tell him to be careful. She no longer had any need for care. She swam around in the feeling of his hands moving across her scalp.

A curious watercolor hung on the wall, just above the light switch. A pair of monstrous charcoal trees grew out of its sky but in reverse: the upper branches were stuck in the clouds, the roots dangling above the earth. Stripes of turquoise and pink and green stretched like contrails across the background, a sunset for the end of the world. A crown of purple had been painted between the trees; it resembled the bottom part of a jaw.

Richard tapped her shoulder. She looked down at the fur between her breasts. In the mirror, she saw that he had cut her hair very short, with fringed, uneven bangs. Given the way she had been shedding, this felt like a natural end to whatever process her body had been engaged in. The sudden absence of hair had exaggerated her features. Everything looked a little swollen, a little sharp.

They stood beside each other in the mirror, arms and hips touching. Cut hair ringed their belly buttons, fringed their collarbones. Their bodies looked like weapons. She detected a subtle shift in her husband's expression, a softening around the eyes and the mouth, an opening up, though the longer she studied their reflections, the more she became unnerved by the thought that those two people were an entirely different couple, trapped inside the glass. She was afraid to move, because if she did and the reflections did not move in synchrony, her suspicion would be confirmed.

It was Richard who broke their stance, by turning and lifting his shirt from the hook. She was careful to turn at the same time, her eyes averted from the mirror, and then she was facing the watercolor: the painting had been hung upside down, the artists' initials in the upper corner as opposed to the bottom. Even after she turned the watercolor right side up she could not banish the inverted forest from her mind.

Wait, she said to Richard, before he could put his shirt back on.

He stopped in the middle of the room. She pulled the curtains across the windows, blotting out the day. She took his shirt from him and draped it over a chair. She held his hands.

He stared at her, his eyes goldish, the corners of his mouth twitching. His lips parted and dewed. She tried very hard to not think upsetting thoughts (she had seen this same body on a hospital table, covered to the throat in a white sheet; she was about to lie down with a ghost or a stranger posing as one). She tried to think only of the heat gathering between their palms.

They collapsed onto the low bed, their skin sticky with hair. She slipped her hands inside his underarms, and then her fingers were sliding across his ribs, over the hard buckle of his belt, down the insides of his thighs. A molten ache announced itself between her legs. Her eyelashes thickened. Her shoulders shook. She was facing away from the door, and if someone was peering through the keyhole, she imagined they would seem like a regular couple—the looker would not see the pressure to vomit growing inside her like a demonic pregnancy or the thief cracking apart the bones in her chest with a crowbar, in pursuit of her heart.

She wished for an invisible third presence in the room, someone who could record everything, so she could later watch the footage and try to understand what had really happened.

Clare, Richard said, wrapping his hands around her skull. Darling.

He sat up and pinned her shoulders to the bed. Every nerve was exposed, alight. She started breathing in shallow gulps, so fast she thought she might die too, sending her consciousness to who-knew-where. His lips wet on her neck, the soft press of muscle and vein, the quench of the ache—and afterward, when she curled up naked and began to sob, broken by overness, he lay behind her and held her close as she wept, something he had never done for her in their former life. There was never an invitation, given the way she kept that second, secret self hidden. Given the way she often seemed to feel so little or felt so much her capacity for expression was overwhelmed—when did she decide that if you couldn't say everything it was better to say nothing at all? Yet this was something he was able to do for her now, in the strangeness of this afterlife.

When she opened the curtains, night had turned the mountains into colossal shadows. She stood naked by the window. She touched the rough spine of hair on the back of her neck. The terrace was no longer empty. It had transformed into a disco, with blue fluorescent lights roaming like search beacons, the music made gentle by distance. People in beige tracksuits were dancing, spotlighted in blue, some in pairs, some gyrating in solitude, unashamed. She had yet to see any visitors in regular clothing and was starting to wonder if she and Richard were the only guests. She thought that this hotel must be offering some kind of cure.

Richard, she said. Come look.

He stood behind her, his hands resting on the shelf of her hips. He reached around and pushed the window open, letting in the mineral air. The music floated up to their room and she could swear she heard Roy Orbison in Spanish. They began to sway like the couples in the beige tracksuits, the back of her head against his warm chest. Little hairs were still stuck to her collarbone. He plucked them up one by one and cast them out.

Do your remember our honeymoon? she asked.

Of course, Richard said.

For their honeymoon, she'd looked into the bed-and-breakfast her parents used to run in Georgia, but it had been razed and converted into a luxury hotel that cost five hundred dollars a night, with private cabanas on the beach. She had wanted to show him the southern coast, and so they went north to Myrtle Beach instead.

On a morning walk, they found a hundred-dollar bill on the beach. They picked it up and raised it to the sun like jewelers examining a stone. In San Diego, the rent was steep. She was between jobs and her husband was saddled with student loans—and, she would discover six months into their marriage, major credit card debt.

We sure didn't budget for *this*, Clare had said as they examined the watermark.

They pocketed the bill and walked on. A little while later they found another one blowing around in the sand, crisp and green and fresh-smelling, like it had just been printed. They felt sure these bills must be fake, even though the watermarks looked authentic enough. Who could possibly lose two hundred dollars?

The weather had been chilly, the beach quiet; on their way back they didn't pass anyone searching for lost money. They took the bills straight to a local bank, where a teller confirmed their authenticity. You just *found* these? the teller had asked, his voice laden with suspicion. They burst back out into the day feeling as though the universe had bestowed on them an omen of great prosperity.

That, or the universe is telling us it's going to be an expensive divorce, Clare had joked, and they'd both laughed. It was only funny because neither of them had enough money to warrant an expensive divorce.

We bought overpriced margaritas, Clare added. We promised to put the rest in savings.

By the window Richard pulled her close.

In her husband's notebook, she had come across a quote from Tzvetan Todorov on the fantastic: "In a world which is indeed our world, the one we know, a world without devils, sylphides, or vampires, there occurs an event which cannot be explained by the laws of this same familiar world." In Myrtle Beach, a world of serendipity had opened up within the familiar, a world that defied the usual laws. She thought such a thing might be happening now, a world opening within another.

Do you think we would have had an expensive divorce? Richard said.

Expensive divorces are for people with children or lots of assets. She snapped her fingers. Ours would have been quick and clean.

She told Richard that she had a theory about marriage, though in truth it was less a theory than an idea that had sprung itself upon her moments ago. The ideal marriage would last for one season. You could have many marriages over the course of your life, if you wanted. Some would be better than others, maybe a person would decide they liked winter marriages the best and summer marriages the least or no marriages at all. The point was that you would get out before you had a chance to change.

There's a name for that, Richard said. It's called a fling.

No, no, said Clare. This would have an entirely different feeling.

A season is no guarantee, Richard said. A person could change in a week or in five minutes' time. Imagine if a boulder came smashing through this window and knocked you straight off this mountaintop. Would you not be changed by the time you reached the bottom?

I might be dead, Clare said.

He spun her around. He clasped her hand, raised it toward the ceiling. Now they were really dancing.

Yes, he said. And that would be quite the change indeed.

They fell asleep together under the thin sheets, the curtains closed tight, the room quiet and dark, but Clare woke in a different place. Something in her bodily wiring had gone wrong. One minute she could not even raise her pinkie finger. The next she felt like she would explode if she did not start running down the beige halls. She was shaking and feverish, burning up and freezing cold. She had once again been loosed in the dark forest and this time she had run straight into a lightless pit with no walls and no floor. She was falling and falling.

She struck herself hard in the face. A fire spread across her skin and then evaporated.

She crashed against the pit's hard bottom, knocking the wind out. She pinched her dry nipples. She squeezed her scaled elbows. She twisted around on the hard mattress. Her calves were cramping. She imagined the eels were back, squirming around inside the muscle.

She struck herself in the face again. She knocked the molar loose and swallowed it whole.

She reached for the man sleeping beside her. The sandpapered knuckles, the dry palms. She spent a long time listening to him breathe. This man was Richard, they were on the island of Cuba, in a hotel known for ecotours and hydromassage—how could this be? It could not be, he was not here, it was impossible, no one could conjure such a thing.

This was the destination her mind kept reaching.

The more she listened to him breathe, or pretend to breathe, the more she felt the widow within, her former self, from her former life, thrashing underneath the surface. The woman who listened to the surgeon explain about the ruptured spleen, the woman who called his parents and then her own, who spoke the unspeakable into the phone, the woman who selected a coffin, the woman who had been given a shovel at the funeral and was asked to participate in smothering her husband in dirt.

The woman who complied.

With each movement of the shovel she had felt she was committing a crime against him.

The widow thrashing within knew she was lying next to an abomination, a delusion of grief, and that any moment she would wake up next to a corpse or alone and so she straddled him. She clawed his shorn hair, her nails piercing his scalp. She groped his face. She wrapped her hands around his throat and squeezed. You're dead, she kept saying, No one is in here. But there were his eyes popping open, wide and afraid. There he was twisting and kicking underneath her. There was his voice shouting her name. She gasped and let go. The wild sweep of his arm knocked her off the bed and they lay panting—husband and wife, assailant and victim, living and not-quite-dead—in the same room until she felt the heat of morning rise up through the wood floor.

PART 3

LAWS UNKNOWN

The traveler was not a peaceful presence in the world. The thought had crossed Clare's mind at the Seahorse, after seeing rooms torn to bits by guests (drawers hanging out like dislocated jaws, shower curtain rods pulled down, soiled balls of sheets—*Get the gloves*, her mother would say) or when a guest left a room so pristine it reeked of a person attempting to pave over misdeed. Like a hotel room was just another body to fuck up. Threatening reviews posted online: "I WOULD BURN THIS PLACE IF I COULD." The moment the plane touched down, the moment the traveler was handed a room key, they were compromised. *I'm not myself here.* Clare had been sold this line and she had sold it. The traveling self was supposed to be temporary, disposed of when it was time to go home—therefore, how could this self be held responsible? But maybe a person became even more themselves when away, liberated from their usual present tense and free to lie. Maybe travel sent all that latent, ancient DNA swimming to the surface. Was that a family of five or a band of marauding conquistadors. Was that a wife or a murderer.

Grief could take the form of violence too, could give a false sense of permission, erase the world around, and that was what frightened Clare most about violence, how transferable it was. After her college boyfriend sent her down the stairs, she had not wished him violence in return. She had not even wanted to file a complaint. She had only wanted to *move on*, to not disturb the soil. Yet when she passed a man climbing a tall ladder, months later, she had wanted to grab the legs and give them a very hard shake, the desire so powerful it had felt like a command.

Lately she had been troubled by the thought that perhaps a life amounted to a sequence of critical looks, and one's time on earth was measured by the willingness to look in the right direction at the right moment. Clearly she lacked such a willingness: her lens had cut away at the wrong times, pivoted in the wrong directions. Systems were hard to shed, and that included the system of her own misdirection, which had taken her entire lifetime to construct. Not what you said or even what you did but where you looked and where you refused to—perhaps that was how a person determined if they were brave or honest or even just reasonably good. The eye was silent and therefore frightfully truthful. The eye did not have to share what it saw with anyone, after all; it did not have to tell a soul.

From the floor, she watched Richard lace up his shoes. She was perpendicular to the bed and could only see his feet, his wrists, his nimble fingers. She blinked and blinked, a lens uselessly shuttering, her cheek pressed flat to the wood. The points of her bones were tender, her muscles jellied. Her brain had been replaced with an orb of steel wool. Her stomach felt like she had spent the night swallowing rocks.

She took a personal inventory and found she was no longer concerned about the suited man with his *Pocket Atlas of Remote Islands*.

That man is gone, she said aloud. I killed him in the night.

The next thing she knew Richard was standing and walking out, his movement summoning her to rise.

Every motion was a fragment, one scarcely connected to the next. She unpeeled herself from the wood floor a single limb at a time. She collected her clothing scattered around the scentless room. She found her wristwatch on the bedside table and was shocked to discover that it was noon, that time had slithered from morning into day. She sat on the edge of the bed to dress. First her watch and her socks and her sneakers, then her clothes. All her movements were out of order.

She raced down the massive stone staircase and through the lobby with the bright art, her backpack banging against her shoulders, and past the patients congregating on the green lawn. They reminded her of very tall birds, flocking to the grass. Despite being surrounded by endless miles of hiking trails, she had yet to see someone in a beige tracksuit actually leave the property.

She went down a steep driveway and then followed a painted wood sign to a trailhead. She spotted Richard in the distance, loping up a brown dirt path halved by a thin spine of grass.

Hey, she said when she caught up to him. *Hey*.

He did not acknowledge her. Movement had been a wall for her husband too, she supposed. During a fit of furious cleaning, she could hover over him and ask any question in the world and it was as though he had erected a shield off which all language bounced; nothing could get through.

Stop, she said. Just stop.

The earth trembled. A tour group on horseback appeared behind them, the animals moving in a slow trot, the riders bouncing in heavy leather saddles. Clare and Richard stepped to the side, into a shallow ditch. She glimpsed a light pink ring around her husband's neck. A man on a black horse held a small camcorder to his face, the lens swooping across Clare and Richard as he narrated his journey aloud. The guide waved as the group ascended the trail. Richard walked on, Claire in pursuit, moving deeper into a forest lush with vegetation, the trail bordered by bamboo and palms. Small birds rustled around in thickets of vine. She heard something rattling in the grass. Some branches were straight as arrows, others serpentine. They passed bushels of pink brugmansias, the inverted trumpets swaying in the wind. Brugmansias were popular in some parts of Florida; the flowers had hallucinogenic properties. A rope bridge led them across a shallow stream and then farther uphill. The path turned rocky and steep. Through the branches the sky was such an intense shade of blue it looked almost fake. A hoax sky.

She heard a mechanical screeching and glimpsed a body in a harness skating across the treetops, and remembered the brochures for ziplining she'd seen in the lobby of the Cure Hotel. Ziplines, cruise ships. What was it about tourists and always wanting to be physically above things?

All the while she felt time ticking down, a heavy pulse in her gut.

They walked until they reached a shallow pool of water that led to a vast limestone cave. Clare felt a little stunned by the cave's beauty, the marvel of it hidden in the trees. It moved her and pained her to see a thing so colossal and so fragile, with its glistening spindles of stalagmite. The mouth was very tall and very slender, the gap shielded by long, thin vines with small, pointy leaves.

A black cable had been secured to the rock, to guide visitors in their climb to the entrance. Richard sloshed through the water and grabbed hold of the cable. Clare watched him pull himself up one rock and then another before disappearing through the tall gap in the limestone. Her own ascent was not so graceful. The cord felt like it had been greased. She scrabbled along the limestone, scraping her knees. Her backpack tugged at her shoulders, arguing in favor of gravity. She heard the sound of falling water. She smelled wet stone and was relieved to have been returned to the world of scent. Once she was inside she found Richard sitting on a large rock, hunched and panting for air. The dead might get to play by their own rules, but even they were not immune to altitude.

She stood at the edge of the cave, her back to the long mouth. Beyond Richard she could make out a dense valley of shadow, and she was uncertain of how much closer she wanted to get.

I want to tell you a story, Richard said in the cave.

His voice was like a glass of cold water poured over her head.

She sat beside him on the rock. She dusted the sweat from her cropped hair.

Years ago, when they were living in San Diego, he had a colleague in the film department who, after his wife died, hired a woman to take her place. Not all the time—just select weekday evenings, the occasional Sunday afternoon. He was not privy to the exact terms, but in this man's presence she went by the same name as his dead wife. She dressed like his wife; she had gotten the same haircut. From office windows, colleagues had seen them strolling around campus, arm in arm, just as this man used to do with his real wife, before she died. It was all very peculiar, but people were slow to criticize—he was, after all, in a state of mourning. But then there were rumors that he was mistreating this woman. He had been seen berating her in restaurants, pulling her roughly down streets. It was unclear if these were things he had done to his former wife, and somehow managed to hide, or things he had always wanted to do but never had. One night, the police came to his home. The rumor was that he had started slapping her during sex and things had gotten worse from there; it sounded like he had nearly tried to kill her, though in the end she declined to press charges. After that, no one saw the stand-in wife anymore. The professor retired and put his house up for sale, his current whereabouts unknown.

This is not a true story, Clare said. I was in San Diego with you. How come I never heard anything about a madman with a stand-in wife?

It happened a few years before we arrived, he said. I know because I took over the professor's office.

That office had been located on the basement level, one barred window to let in minimal light, not enough to keep a philodendron alive. To her, it was a nondescript space, no obvious signs of menace, though now she wondered if this is where the department had stashed the professors they did not particularly care for.

My point here is that the grieving are very dangerous, Richard said. They are like injured animals with fearsome claws, bloodied and pushed into a corner.

Okay, said Clare.

They are deranged, he continued. They shouldn't be let out of the house. Immediately after the funeral some sort of waiting period should be instituted, a period of confinement. It is a matter of public safety.

Clare lifted her right leg and stepped down on his foot.

She said, Your point has been made.

From the inside the cave entrance was guarded by long lime-stone stalagmites that cast shadows onto the rocks. She felt like they were sitting within a creature, in the soft tissue just behind the jaw.

I should have expected something like this, Richard said. I should have been prepared. For months and months, you'd been acting so strangely.

I had been acting strangely?

You were the one, she said. You were the one who started acting strangely.

The conversation made her feel like she was standing in front of the cave wall and pushing against the stone; something about it was too big, too solid and difficult to move.

Richard told her that wasn't right at all. He had only been trying to get to the bottom of what was happening to his wife. Did she really not remember how, in February, she came back from Omaha and didn't speak a complete sentence for days? At first he thought she might be having an affair, though later he began to suspect something even more complicated and grave. This evolution in suspicion started after she fell into a similar state of speechlessness upon receiving a piece of mail from her father. A thin envelope that she opened in the bathroom. She'd refused to say what had been inside.

No, Clare said. This is not right at all.

It *is*, he insisted.

No. She covered her eyes.

I am not capable.

No decision has been made.

Richard pulled her hand away from her face, one finger at a time.

They walked deeper into the cave, climbing over sharp rocks and ledges of limestone, stepping across blankets of pebble, the surfaces glossed by water, and silver wedges of silt. She had expected the cave to grow darker, and that with each step they would be committing to move into this darkness together, no place or maybe every place to hide now, but instead currents of natural light brightened the cave floor. The sound of falling water grew louder, a rushing that burned between her ears. She thought that this was what the last year of their marriage had been like. A deafening current all around, drowning out their small and deceitful voices. She watched their hunched shadows creep across the stone walls.

As it turned out, the cave had been more like a tunnel. They crawled through a circular opening, the rough mouth ringed with light, and then up a slick stone footpath. Outside they found themselves standing on the bank of a swift emerald river. The air was even cooler and thinner, the vegetation denser, the treetops transformed into canopies of leaf and vine, the branches braided together by a light fog; they appeared to have reached a higher plane of elevation. She could see where the river charged downhill, the mane of white froth churning in the distance. A waterfall had been the source of the rushing.

To celebrate the first year of their marriage, she and Richard spent a weekend in Las Vegas. They lost money at blackjack, woke in the morning with latticed memories: neon shards glimpsed through cab windows; her husband moving behind her in the hotel shower, his hands on her hips; sinking into the sticky softness of a booth in some nocturnal bar. Their hotel was north of the Strip and the room had been very cheap. The cops turned up the first night, the lights soaking the plastic blinds in red; there had been a fight in the parking lot. She found a pink wig sitting in the small microwave. They had needed this cheap room in order to have enough funds for the flight and the drinks and the rental car.

Outside Las Vegas they passed a casino, she remembered, and a Baptist church and, to their great surprise, a white stucco opera house called the Amargosa. A little while later the Stovepipe Wells General Store appeared like a movie set, with a covered wagon and a hitching post, the last thing they would see for many miles.

Richard would never have wanted to go to Las Vegas on his own. On their first night, he had remarked that this place was fun with the right company but could easily be made nightmarish by solitude. Clare, for her part, would have never wanted to go into Death Valley on her own. Florida had trained her to be skittish around the natural world; you never knew where or when a snake might turn up. For these reasons, she blamed their marriage, a force field with its own design, for what ended up happening.

She remembered how they had rolled down the windows on their way into Death Valley. They stuck their hands into the air. They went fast along the straight highway. They felt like outlaws. They passed signs warning of EXTREME HEAT and Clare looked at Richard and winked and said, They *must* be talking about us.

In the Badwater Basin, they pulled over to take photos of where the salt had made a honeycomb pattern in the sand. She thought the ridges looked like animal spines and kept this thought to herself without knowing why.

They returned to the car and continued on, past the Funeral Mountains. They followed a sign for a lookout. They turned off the highway, drove up a short, steep road. Dust swarmed the rental car. Desert rock crunched under the tires. At one point, the car stuttered, but her husband gunned the engine and they leapt up to the top; it felt like they were driving right into the sun. From the lookout, the salt basin below appeared extraterrestrial, part of the barren, pocked landscapes rovers photographed on Mars. They took photos on the edge of the lookout, and in one, because his brother had not yet ended his life by jumping from a bridge, Richard feigned the posture of a person about to fall.

When they got back into their car, it would not start. They popped the hood: the engine hissed, thin streams of smoke rose from deep inside the gears. Clare touched the dark curve of a tube and gasped when the heat stung her fingers. They had two liters of water, a bag of macadamia nuts, and three apples. No GPS, no cell service, no memory of the last mile marker. It was late afternoon and a hundred degrees. They decided to try to hitch a ride, so they skidded down the short hill to the road, the sun beating against their shoulders. They brought one liter of water, and it was gone before they reached the bottom, bodies radiating dust.

A car piloted by teenagers, heavy metal escaping through cracked windows, roared past and then nothing for a long time, so they climbed back up to the lookout, which proved much harder than going down, and collapsed in the backseat of the rental car. They foolishly ate all the macadamia nuts. They gulped down the second liter of water and it wasn't enough— she wanted more and more. They fell asleep. When she woke, the sun had been devoured. They left the car, shaking the stiffness from their bodies; never before had they seen such impenetrable night. From the lookout they watched the highway for passing headlights. An animal howled. They lay down on the steaming hot roof and looked up at a dense, inky sky. Where were the stars? She would think about that desert dark when she walked Havana at night, the streets half-lit or unlit once away from the tourist sites; never in a city had she looked up and seen so many stars.

Splayed out on the car Clare had felt a growing fury. Why had they not brought maps and more water and food? Why had they driven up to the lookout in the first place—whose idea had that been? She imagined he was thinking a similar set of thoughts beside her, even if they too went unexpressed. Silence facilitated blame, she would decide later. In the absence of another person's account, the story you invented for yourself went unchallenged.

We just need to make it to morning, she said, her voice thin and unconvincing in the desert.

If we do, we will have survived our first natural disaster.

Man-made, if we want to get technical about it, she said.

I'll amend to our first disaster *in* nature.

Amendment accepted.

All night she had been telling jokes. Back then she loved jokes, the worse the better; she could remember only a few of her old favorites now.

A man and a woman walk into the desert, she said, then stopped because she didn't yet have a punch line.

Later that night, they crawled into the backseat of the car that now felt like a coffin and fell asleep on top of each other. When they woke, the car was shaking. They couldn't see out the windows; the world had erected a screen between them and the outdoors. Dust was blowing around inside, in her mouth and up her nose. Her face was pressed against his ribs. The wind shoved the car around on the lookout and then they were rocking backward and then they were sliding, trunk first, hood rearing. They screamed as the car sailed down the hill, banging over rocks and brush, and came to rest on the highway shoulder, two particles cast into outer space, two particles spinning apart, as a void opened beneath them and then, by some miracle, decided to close.

At dawn, they were rescued by an old woman driving a jeep. They were sitting on the hood of the rental car, caked in sweat and dust, bruised and aching, when she materialized on the road. She wore her silver hair in a long braid and a red T-shirt that featured Hulk Hogan waving an American flag.

The woman had no air-conditioning, broken seat belts, and one condition. She was on her way to the Baptist church, and if they wanted a ride to Vegas, they would have to wait until the service ended, and that was how Clare and Richard came to find themselves sitting in the back of the desert church, holding a linen prayer book they never opened. Her palms bled sweat into the blue binding. The scent of cigarette smoke rose from the carpeting. Whoever was in charge of keeping up this church had a habit.

At the end of the service, the pastor told everyone to get on their knees and shut their eyes because it was time for those who wished to be saved to beg for forgiveness. Clare and Richard did not kneel or close their eyes, and after a long silence, just when she was thinking no one would come forward, a young man with a cowlick slipped from his pew and crawled to the front, followed by a woman in a denim dress, her legs pushing against the carpet, and then a man in a belt with a long knife attached, who crept like a dog. On all fours, head hung.

All of a sudden she felt her husband gathering himself, preparing to make a move. He shot up from the pew and then he was on his knees, crawling fast toward the altar. She had never heard Richard express a religious sentiment—was that even her husband up there? The pastor walked the row of kneelers, touched the top of every head. He bent over and whispered into each person's ear.

After the service, they gulped apple juice in the church basement, making small talk with the other congregants, who were all polite enough to not comment on the fact that Clare and Richard looked like they had just climbed out of a ditch.

Danger keeps a marriage alive, the old woman said in the church parking lot. My late husband and I used to take wrestling classes together. People thought we'd go easy on each other because we were husband and wife, but it was just the opposite. Once he fractured my ribs. Once I gave him two black eyes.

Clare supposed this theory hinged on both people having the same idea about what constituted danger.

The woman squared her shoulders and turned her hands to claws. She mimicked facing an opponent. She began to grapple with the air, or perhaps with her dead husband, pushing and grunting, her silver braid swinging, until she flipped the invisible opponent onto their back. She stomped the gravel, sending up a white cloud of dust.

Tourists have died in Death Valley, Richard would say back in Las Vegas, when Clare wanted an explanation. They were huddled in the small shower, scrubbing each other's bodies raw with bar soap and a washcloth. Usually such a disaster began with some minor mishap: they got a little lost, they miscalculated the weather, their car broke down, *and then.* But they made it out. They were alive. It was a miracle they'd not been badly injured. That was the best he could do to explain why he had gone to the altar.

What doesn't kill you makes you stronger, Clare said, with bitterness.

What doesn't kill you leaves you alive, Richard countered.

She spat water onto the floor. What doesn't kill you only leaves you feeling broken and insane.

He placed his hands on her shoulders and pressed her gently to the wall. She felt the water slap the tops of her feet. The fat vein throbbed. He said going up to the altar had just been an impulse and that it did not mean anything.

Clare did not tell him how left behind she had felt in the pew, a door slammed shut in her face and now she would have to figure out how to crack it back open—or not. He let go of her shoulders. She lathered the washcloth and rubbed white circles on his chest. The earliest betrayals stung the sharpest.

She imagined fashioning his leaving into a joke, her own underhanded form of revenge: *A man and a woman walk into a church in the desert. One of them walks out with a brand-new soul and the other gets left in the dust.*

Richard told her that at the altar he'd opened his eyes, even though the pastor had said not to, and he couldn't stop looking at the pastor's shoes: black and cheap, the heels worn down to rubber discs.

They were the shoes of a low-level bureaucrat, he said. They were the shoes of unemployed professors at academic conferences. They were the shoes people get buried in.

In the shower, they did not yet know that soon they would be deciding on burial shoes for his brother.

By then her brother-in-law's descent was well under way. They had become fluent in the awful numerical language of statistics; Clare felt these figures colluded in acts of dehumanization and this made the numbers feel evil to her. Seventeen percent of patients diagnosed with traumatic brain injury reported suicidal thoughts: this was the first evil-seeming statistic Clare and Richard had memorized together, after his brother fell while on a construction job in La Jolla. The fall was the disaster that gave way to all the other disasters: Tegretol, joblessness, homelessness. The majority of suicidal TBI patients were men between twenty-five and thirty-five. He was a year away from leaping from the bridge, and in that aftermath she would feel more generously toward her husband's crawl to the altar. She would wonder if a part of Richard had felt the future ghost of his brother up there, calling him forward. She did not yet know that they would spend much of their marriage bracing for departures they could not see coming.

The last time she and Richard visited her parents in Florida, a month before he was struck by the car and killed, she had imagined that her father might be feeling what she had felt in the desert car, in Death Valley, a long slide into the void. For him, though, there was no chance of the void ever closing; it would only get wider. They were sitting on a couch in the house that would soon be only her mother's house. A sour smell was trapped in the wallpaper; the windows were fogged. She asked her father if he remembered her story about the car that broke down in the desert and he frowned and kept saying the word "car" like he had never heard of such a thing before. His twisted his hands together, his wrists dappled with small blue bruises, and began to shout, Car? Car? What car?

What were you doing in Havana?

On the riverbank, Richard's voice sliced through the thunder of her own thoughts. The back of his shirt was printed with sweat marks in the shape of claws. They were sitting close to the rushing water. On the opposite side a slender trail curved around the river, the path bumpy with rocks. A sharp sunlight had burned away the mist.

I wanted to see the movie, she said. I wanted to meet Yuniel Mata.

She did not tell him that if she just kept circling place after place, if her migratory pattern could expand, then she might stand a chance of escaping this monstrous-feeling inner life, this tangle of woolly midnight thoughts. She could turn herself into a ghost, and ghosts weren't expected to be anything but bystanders, their work of being alive already done.

She did not know how to grieve her husband's death or her father's decline or the choice each day carried her closer to, the choice she was wholly unprepared to make—or would turn out to be more prepared than any person should be.

She did not know how to grieve in the context of her life.

Bullshit, Richard said. No one gets on a plane to see a movie.

Everyone dies at the end, she said, except the hero's daughter.

In the end, Agata Alonso's character had escaped the ravaged city by motorboat. She had lost the zombie tape in a failed attempt to save her father, but she had held on to her own life.

Richard took off his shoes and peeled the socks from his long white feet. He cuffed his pants and waded into the river, just past his ankles, the water darkening the khaki hems.

Never give away the ending, he said from the river. Never ever.

She heard a rustling and, through the bushes on the opposite side of the water, she glimpsed an animal stamping down the path. She thought of the escaped ostrich and imagined the creature having found its way into the Escambray Mountains, where it could roam about in peace, free of pens and gawking tourists. The animal cleared the foliage and turned out to be not one but two: a pair of bleating brown goats.

The mind contained a million half-open doors and they could become closed or swing open at any time, by virtue of remembering or forgetting or illness or petrified avoidance. On the riverbank, she felt one blow open.

I want to talk about the notebook, Clare said.

She felt the moist ground seeping through her shorts. The river was funneling a hooked branch toward the froth; for a moment it had looked like an arm.

Richard waded farther out, the water swallowing his knees.

The notebook, Clare said again.

When she had opened the little red notebook in Richard's office, she'd immediately recognized her father's hand. The first entry was dated a week after his diagnosis. The last entry was dated in September and barely legible, the letters dropping down the lined pages like tears. She could picture a small parcel mixed in with the bills and the takeout flyers and the reminder postcards from the doctor and the dentist. From the postmark she had been able to track her whereabouts to Iowa City. All those months she had been ignorant of the record her father had been keeping, ignorant that he had entrusted it to her, ignorant of her husband's interception. Ignorant of the investigation he had launched and then left unfinished.

Clare stood and stepped carefully into the river, as though the stones might be concealing a trap. The cold bit at her ankles. Above she heard the distant scream of the zipline. A harnessed body whipped over a canopy, legs kicking.

Why did you take it? She sloshed toward Richard, the coolness closing around her knees. Why didn't you tell me?

Blood pounded through her body. Her armpits burned.

Richard sank down into the river, like he was getting ready for a leisure swim.

The water was at her waist, and she felt the pull of the current.

Ever since she took a call from her father in a hotel room in Omaha, ever since that first envelope from him turned up in New Scotland and she opened it to find a business card with a name and a number—

Ever since all of that she had felt like her body was being remade one cell at a time. Changing.

The fog cleared and the sun dumped light through the tree branches. In the river her husband's head was a brilliant flame, the burning end of a lit match. His distance, his silence, felt like a taunt. She raised her backpack over her head.

She called out *Richard* and it was as though the sound of his own name drove him away, given the speed with which he dove underwater, swam fast toward the churning froth, and then slipped like quicksilver over the falls.

Clare stumbled forward, and by then she was too far into the current to argue with its logic, that perfect, thoughtless force that did not care about human want. A band of pressure formed around her hips. Her knees bent, her toes lifted, her field of vision was overtaken by tree and sky. She raised her backpack higher. When it was over, she would have no memory of whether she had screamed and thrashed as the current dragged her toward the froth or if she had just let it happen, if she had let the river breathe her in and then breathe her out, straight down the falls and into a turquoise pool, her heart escaping through her throat.

For six months after her brother-in-law died, her husband had dreams where he thought his dead brother was calling in the middle of the night, and then once, around two in the morning, the phone started to ring for real. Richard answered, disoriented, freshly launched from sleep. He collapsed on the carpet, *hello hello hello*, while Clare kneeled beside him on the bed, clutching the covers.

No one was on the line.

After her husband died, she had dreams where he was ringing the doorbell in the middle of the night, and then once it actually happened, also around two in the morning: she was awake and the doorbell was ringing for real. She ran downstairs and flung the door open, even though any Final Girl would know opening up your house in the middle of the night was an invitation to be murdered—but nothing, so far as she could tell, was out there.

She wondered what she would dream about after her father was gone.

By the time Clare found her way back to the Cure Hotel, the afternoon sun shone down on the mountains and her clothes had hardened into an exoskeleton. Patients in their beige tracksuits still populated the lawn. One woman raised her hand in greeting.

Clare walked straight through the lobby and to the terrace, where the bar had been overtaken by a group of birders. There was an older couple in sunbonnets; two women, newlyweds; adult twin sisters, American; and a man who appeared to be unaccompanied. They were all recounting the glory of having seen the bee hummingbird, a species exclusive to Cuba, smaller than a bumblebee and thus very difficult to spot.

The woman in the sunbonnet asked Clare if she had come from the trails, and for a moment her heart surged, thinking this woman might be about to tell her that they had found a man roaming the forest, sopping and barefoot and looking for a person who fit her description.

We heard the most terrible screaming, the woman said, her voice alight with excitement. I thought we were going to find a dead body out there, like in a Nelson DeMille novel.

Nelson DeMille has never set a novel in Cuba, said her husband.

Well, the woman said, *I* think he should.

The birders collected a round of magenta daiquiris, and the pairs drifted over to round tables stationed under green umbrellas, leaving the unaccompanied man adrift on the terrace. Before joining the others, one of the newlyweds put her hand on Clare's shoulder and asked, gently, if she was aware that she was bleeding from her forehead.

Clare took a seat and ordered a straight vodka from a bartender in a maroon vest and heavy eyeliner. She soaked a paper napkin in water and pressed it to the short, bloodied crown at her hairline.

After she swam to the pool's limestone edge and heaved her body onto dry land, she had found herself on yet another winding trail. She had looked back at the falls and seen that she had not dropped very far at all. The greatest danger would have been bashing her head on a rock.

Wet footprints stamped across the brown dirt. Ahead she had glimpsed Richard moving through the trees.

She'd imagined scurrying back up the riverbank and gathering his shoes, his socks. She'd imagined stuffing his socks in her pockets and wearing his shoes on her hands, marching through the forest and clapping the soles together, flushing him out.

On the trail, the falls churning behind her, she had clutched her sopping backpack to her chest and remembered the white box, the reel of film. She clawed through her pack; the wet cardboard fell apart in her hands. She pinched a thin plastic tab between her thumb and forefinger, pulled out a few frames, all dewed with river. She mopped them dry on her shirt.

She had looked again toward the forest. Richard was still visible. Even without her binoculars she could see him stepping through the trees.

She had raised the reel to the sky.

I lost it in a shark attack, a voice said.

The unaccompanied man appeared next to her. He opened his mouth wide, baring his teeth.

Lost what?

She finished her vodka and asked for another. Language felt soft on her tongue. A poster from Paradiso Cuba was tacked to the wall behind the bar, an empty blue lounge chair on a white beach, shaded by a thatched umbrella. She wondered why the chair was empty. Perhaps so that the viewer could visualize themselves sitting there and looking out, with their secret subjective eye.

My left ear, the man said. His collarbone was a ridge across his chest. His cheeks were padded with dove-gray stubble.

She squinted at the side of his head. If her vision could be trusted, his left ear was exactly where it should be.

But I can see your ear right there. She pointed at his temple.

Don't be fooled! It's a fake.

He detached his left ear in one swift movement, like twisting open a bottle. He tossed the fake ear around in his hands. He placed it on the table. He started telling Clare to touch it, go ahead and touch it, and when she did she was repulsed by the way it felt just like a real ear: the warm squish of skin, the firm line of cartilage.

The bartender sighed and turned away from this spectacle, annoyed yet unsurprised, as though this man had been removing his ear on this terrace every night for years.

A tiny green frog hopped across the bar, heart wild under the skin.

A hot wind raked the treetops.

On the trail, she had squinted at one of the frames and was able to make out a figure—a woman, a sight. She was standing at a kitchen sink, head bowed, as though she was staring at something in the basin, as though a whole world might be contained in there. Clare brought the frame closer and realized she was looking at herself, in her parents' kitchen in Florida. She was being viewed from a strange angle, perhaps through a window. She had not felt the weight of the camera, had not felt the weight of her husband's eye behind the lens, and she had felt shamed by her blindness, a hot clench in her heart.

I prefer the mountains to the beaches, the man told her, a lit cigarette drooping between his fingers. The beaches are infested with crabs. Last winter, I stayed at a seaside resort with salsa classes on the beach and before long everyone was running away from the crabs.

What are you even doing here? she asked him.

I am escaping the Canadian winter. He exhaled through his teeth. I live in the town of Regina. Do you know how cold it gets in the town of Regina?

He sang the name Regina. The hot orange tip of his cigarette resembled the fuse on a bomb.

He winked. On the other hand, the seaside resort was, as they say, an all-inclusive. I got two marriage proposals in a week.

Don't worry, he said, winking again. You're too old for me.

Sir, she thought. Don't make me murder you.

She eyed the fork someone had left on the bar.

He asked Clare what her story was, in a tone that indicated he had zero interest in her story and was merely trying to keep the conversation afloat, and so she started in on elevators, the one arena in which she still felt a modicum of certainty.

Hoists appeared in the third century. The first electric elevator was built by the German inventor Werner von Siemens. A single steel elevator cable is strong enough to hold a car. Her favorite elevators in the world? The Hammetschwand in Switzerland and the AquaDom in Germany. The Sky Tower in New Zealand. The Yokohama in Japan.

She imagined cables snapping, a wild spray of black tentacles.

She imagined a car exploding as it struck the bottom of the shaft.

He looked at her, his head wreathed with smoke. Behind the bar the woman in the maroon vest appeared to be setting something on fire. The man clasped his ear to his heart. Clare recalled the time her mother found a prosthetic finger in a recently vacated room. You'd think someone would come back for that, her father had remarked, but no. They kept it in the reception desk; once a new employee mistook it for a pencil eraser.

Hey, what's the matter with you? the man asked as though he was noticing for the first time that something was not quite right with this woman alone at the bar, half-drunk and bleeding.

As she stared at the image of herself on film, Clare had imagined stepping into the frame and taking that past self, that self who no longer existed, by the hand and walking her straight into her own future.

When the sun shifted in the sky and the frame went translucent, she had turned to the forest, the strip of film held to her face like a view finder.

Richard was gone. Nothing but sepia air between the trees.

At Albany Memorial, less than fifty days ago, the surgeon had walked into the waiting room and Clare had felt the room tilt as he took her arm and said nothing of Final Girls. Instead he said, Maybe if we had gotten to him sooner, maybe we could have done more for your husband then, but the way it happened we just ran out of time.

It's your face. At the bar, the man from Regina pressed a hand to his stubbled cheek.

He said, You look like somebody just died.

Clare returned to Havana alone.
        She hitched a ride with the American twins, who were leaving the Cure Hotel for Cienfuegos. The twins had freckled noses and bright blue eyes. They were tall and tan; when they met Clare in the lobby, the backpacks hitched to their shoulders looked as long and heavy as sleds. One of them had a birthmark in the shape of a butterfly on her bicep. They were traveling on a pair of black motorbikes.

Americans have to stick together, said one twin.

Especially women, said the other.

The twins fist-bumped each other and then Clare.

Clare went with the woman with the birthmark. She mounted the bike and wrapped her arms around the woman's firm waist. Her neck smelled floral. It had been a long time since Clare had touched another woman with such intimacy, the motorbike now an interior zone of vulnerability.

The sisters wore headlamps around their helmets, the beams

cutting through the shadows of early evening. The mountain road blazed with light. A rock, the golden eyes of an animal, a quivering plant—the lights seized these fragments, held them for a moment, and then bumped along. The bikes accelerated into a dense wind and then dove downhill, bounding over a large pothole.

At the bottom of the road, the sea.

The water was like a chart mapping variations of the color blue: turquoise in the shallows, royal in the depths. Clare saw the white blast of waves striking shore and gulls crossing over, bobbing stiffly in the air, as though they were not real birds but decoys supported by invisible strings. This world of nature that would push on.

On the bike, Clare sweated, her stomach cramped. She drank down the salted air. She felt like the water was chasing them.

In the final sliver of daylight, the sisters wanted to stop at a slender beach. A few families were huddled under thatched umbrellas. Two children darted in and out of the tide, shrieking about the temperature. She took out her binoculars and caught whitecaps in the shape of claws.

The sisters chained their bikes to the wood fence that surrounded a bereft snack bar. They hiked up their pants and ran screaming into the sea.

They did not come back alone, but in the company of two young men, also looking for a ride to Cienfuegos. The men were muscled and handsome in their sleeveless T-shirts and denim shorts, seawater dripping from their hair. They spoke to the twins in German, a language Clare recognized but could not understand, and the twins spoke to the men in English—yet somehow the four of them were able to make themselves understood.

Sorry, one twin said to Clare, her feet bright with sea.

You can find a taxi over there, said the twin with the birth-mark. She pointed in the direction of the snack bar.

She watched the twins unchain the bikes and drag them back toward the road, the two men trotting along in their wake.

In Cienfuegos, the streets were long and straight, the southern edge kissed by a large bay. When the taxi dropped her at the station, it was late and the next train did not leave until the following afternoon. She spent the night in the station, though she did not sleep, did not so much as close her eyes. She sat upright on a wood bench until it was time to board, and then she rode the French Train through the day and into the night, slumped over like she'd been shot. She thought about things she had not thought about in a very long time, like her first memory of wonder, which had occurred in the Blue Ridge Mountains, at the age of five. She was in the car with her parents. They were winding up a mountainous road, in the early morning. She could not remember their exact destination; she remembered only the smoky fog nestled in the ridges, as though the mountains were being consumed by their own breath, and the voice of her father telling her that God did not live in the cosmos, like many people thought, but inside of things, inside trees and mountains; it was, as Clare had thought, breath. Her mother, who was driving, pointed out that the fog came from the atmosphere, not from the earth, and then Clare's father rolled down the window and told his daughter to smell the air and she did; she craned her neck and sniffed that thing people called air—something that no one could see but that everyone felt all the time—like an eager dog. She re-membered smelling pine and tar and salt and animal, but the pine was the strongest, the scent that overlay the other scents, and for every year after she would not be able to smell pine without thinking, fleetingly, about the breath of God.

By the time her parents retired, Clare had read every single Trip-Advisor review of the Seahorse. After the Cat 3 hurricane, two of the evacuated guests gave the inn one star, on account of the storm ruining their vacation. One of these reviewers had spelled "hurricane" with a single *r*. Clare had logged many complaints about the absence of a swimming pool, even though there was no promise of a swimming pool on the website or anywhere else and the Atlantic Ocean was less than a hundred feet away—the problem was that people tended to equate Florida with swimming pools. The most scathing one-star review was titled "FINE PLACE IF YOU DON'T MIND LOSING YOUR WILL TO LIVE."

The root of "tourism" sprang from the Saxon word *Torn*. Later *Torn* became *Torn-us*, "what gives turns," and *Torn-are*, "to give turns," roughly translating into "a departure with the intention of returning." *I could stay here forever* was something people felt free to say only when they knew there was no such possibility.

The night of the hurricane, Clare had been outwardly frightened by the lashing rain and inwardly frightened by the presence of Ellis Martin. In response, her father suspended her usual bedtime. He announced a dinner of chocolate bars and Cokes. By nine the electricity was out. They played charades, taking turns spotlighting each other with a flashlight. Her father performed certain guests—the northerners who had never seen a lizard or a flying cockroach; the rowdy spring breakers. Ellis Martin pretended to be celebrities unknown to Clare, though her father recognized her impressions right away; she was shut out of their language. Clare was a dog running on the beach. She was driving a car. She thought of the boy, visiting from Michigan, that lifeguards had saved from a riptide that summer. She raised her hands straight over her head. She turned in a circle. She was drowning.

Look at you, her father had said. You're a ballerina. You're dancing.

He had always been a man of imagination.

When it was time to sleep, her father put sheets on the living room couch, his bed for the night, and showed Ellis Martin into the master bedroom. He left a lantern flashlight in Clare's room, with an extra set of batteries. He said she could leave it on all night, if she was afraid. He closed her door and for a long while she heard nothing but the besieged apartment, the whistle and creak of it fending off the storm.

In the middle of the night, she was awoken by the sound of a door opening and closing, two gentle clicks, low laughter through the walls. She turned away from the noise and closed her eyes and reemerged hours later, into the daylit quiet. The storm was over and Ellis Martin was gone. Her father claimed she had found a tow truck that morning, though Clare had already started to suspect the car trouble had been a story, constructed for her benefit.

That afternoon, she helped her father unboard the windows. After he pulled out the nails, he handed them to her and she returned them to a cardboard container the size of a matchbox. In twenty-four hours, the inn would reopen for business; the owners in Atlanta would be pleased. That Christmas her parents would receive a bonus.

LAURA VAN DEN BERG

Did you know, her father said, that when your mother was a child, when she was exactly your age, she fell into a well and no one found her for two days?

Clare did not know.

The well was deep in the woods, he went on. Her parents thought she had been abducted or that she had run away or gotten into an accident. Imagine being down there. Imagine hearing nothing human for miles. Imagine looking up and watching the sky go dark.

Clare could imagine it, at least a little. During the storm, she had felt like they'd dropped down into another layer; they were no longer on the exterior of the earth but somewhere just below. She had always thought her mother, with her personality of surfaces, and whatever those surfaces were eliding, was the parent who had the capacity to shock Clare, to do something that might one day scare the daylights out of her.

No one will ever know what passed between them, her father said next. He kneeled in front of a window. He wiped his forehead with his wrist.

Between who? Clare squeezed her small fist around a nail.

Your mother and the well.

Clare never saw Ellis Martin again, and when she'd read her name on the business card her father had mailed her, she'd felt like someone was dropping ice cubes down her shirt. She had no idea they had remained in touch, had maintained a relationship; clearly her father's own second, secret self had kept busy. She could not even see Ellis Martin's face clearly, it had been so long. She could not imagine her as an older woman.

As it happened, Ellis Martin was still a doctor—an anesthesiologist. Her father did not want to go on past a certain point and he wanted his desired course of action to remain a secret; he felt his own wife was not to be trusted with his wishes. His daughter, on the other hand; he knew what she was made of. When the time came, Ellis Martin was the person Clare was to call—what she had agreed to provide would be the sickle, Clare the hand.

The train swayed gently on the tracks. It woke the goats from their sleep. Clare wandered toward unconsciousness, her mind circling back to something she had witnessed the week before Richard died. She happened to be standing at a window when she saw him returning from his evening walk. The street was dark and he was visible to her only when he passed under the beam of a streetlight—vanish, appear, vanish, appear—but still she was certain of what she saw: he was walking the same as he had before the great change took hold, brisk and impatient, no time for anything but his own progress through the night.

She had witnessed this sight and felt relieved. Whatever it was he had been going through, he was starting to come out of it. Maybe he would be fine.

She now wondered if, on this walk, he had been thinking the same thing about her.

Eight days later he was dead.

Somewhere in the province of Matanzas, Clare opened her eyes to a train car dark and careening.

The seats shook. The windows rattled like loose teeth. A suitcase plummeted from the overhead rack and smashed open, spilling wrinkled clothes and Polaroid photos that took flight around the car.

The train heaved, hurling bodies against seatbacks, and then stilled. A throb clustered in the center of her forehead. Clare felt her face and her stomach and her knees. She felt around the window; a Polaroid was stuck to the glass. She peeled it away. Not enough light to make out an image. For what felt like a long time, no one tried to escape the car. The passengers sat panting inside the pitch-darkness, as though everyone was afraid that if they moved the train might answer in kind.

Finally the woman sitting in front of Clare broke the stillness. She stood, a hand outstretched, grasping at shadow. Soon more passengers rose to their feet and stumbled down the unlit aisles, stepping over bags and yanking open doors. One woman crawled through an open window; Clare saw her ankles kicking before she tumbled out and onto the earth. Adults in the train passed children to adults on the ground. She smelled smoke. She was afraid to leave her seat. She watched a man break a lock on a door with a small ax.

Across the aisle, an old man struggled to rise. With her father, she had become practiced at shouldering the weight of a grown man (and there would be much more practice to come) and so for once she knew what to do. She squatted beside him. He was folded over in his seat, murmuring a name. She lashed herself to his body, fingers laced across his breastbone, elbows tight against his ribs. His underarms wet and hot on her skin. She pulled and up he went.

Outside two women in skirts rushed toward Clare and the stranger leaning against her. They took his hands and led him away. She watched the women pat his snowy head, lick their fingers and wipe his face, in the manner of adults working to make a child presentable. His daughters. A wind shook the trees. People stood in huddles, or sat on the ground, in the dull glow of travel-size flashlights and lanterns and cell phone screens and moon. Her hearing felt muted, as though they were all underwater. Night bugs rose from the grass, flitting through streams of light. She noticed a few passengers taking videos on their phones.

The front car had vaulted from the tracks, twisted like a head on a freshly broken neck, and now the entire machine sat steaming in the night. A derailment, though it could have been much worse.

Clare could not make herself stand still, she walked circles in the grass, she kept grabbing at the front of her shirt, the straps of her pack. She watched the two women lead their father through the grass and over a hill. Other passengers had taken to walking down the tracks. A man carrying a briefcase vanished into the night, and as Clare watched his leaving, an even more radical form of movement began to seem possible, one that meant she would never be heard from as Clare again, offering instead a name that would fill people with the slight suspicion that it was not, in fact, her own.

She noticed a man in a dark suit sitting in the grass, smoking a cigarette and reading a book, aided by a tiny flashlight. She recognized his posture, his heavy mustache. She felt certain he was reading *The Pocket Atlas of Remote Islands*, but as she drew closer she saw that he was wearing a crew member's uniform and reading a dense manual titled *Protocolos de Emergencia*, turning the pages with urgency.

Emergency protocols.

On a small rise, a woman in a khaki dress and a baseball cap waved a miniature American flag; people were congregating around her. The gathering people hugged each other, rested hands on shoulders. Clare walked over to the group, counting packs of all kinds: backpacks, fanny packs, hip packs. A woman thrust her phone to the sky, in search of a signal, a circular neck pillow fastened to the straps of her shoulder bag. A tour group had been riding on the train.

At the Seahorse, someone would occasionally turn up at the complimentary continental breakfast who was not a guest. One woman, a local, slipped by three times before Clare's parents caught on. She wore a white terrycloth dress and a gold ankle bracelet, her shoulders pink from the sun. Clare's mother had said she really looked the part. It was remarkable, truly, what appearance could make permissible.

Clare fixed herself to the outskirts of the group. It was a large tour, maybe forty people, all touching each other, all chattering on. She would draw no attention. When the guide led them away from the train, Clare followed, over the tracks, down a sloped dirt road, and into a pair of waiting vans.

A quick headcount, no extra seats. If left standing she would be outed. She hurried straight to the back of the van and into the tiny bathroom. She sat on the toilet seat and locked the door. The walls shuddered as the van drove away.

Through the door she heard a man and a woman arguing over whether they could now finally agree that there was such a thing as *too* much authenticity.

The vans dropped them in a dark square, not far from the sea, the air bowed with water. They were in a town on the coast, Clare did not catch the name. They followed the guide to a small hotel. While the room keys were being given out, Clare slunk up the stairs, past a black-and-white cat, a real one this time. The tip of its tail flicked back and forth. The cat paused in front of Clare and flashed its teeth, the incisors sharp as needles.

In the hotel by the sea, there were no elevators. No bar. She considered what kind of elevator she would have advised for this place: perhaps a birdcage installed with UltraRope, so it would look old but go very fast. In a hallway on the third floor, she found a rotary phone sitting on a stool. She would station herself here, and if anyone passed, she could pretend to be making a call. She picked it up and listened to the dial tone. She slid down the wall, the earpiece pressed against her chest. At two in the morning, she dialed her parents' number, collect.

Hello, her mother answered. What's wrong.

That was how her mother had been answering any calls that came in after ten, ever since Clare had phoned in the middle of the night to tell her Richard had been killed. *Hello. What's wrong.*

She listened to her mother breathe on the phone. She imagined a polished surface, reflecting and reflecting. At least her mother had always kept her secrets to herself. She had not ever asked her child to carry them.

It's me, Clare said.

It's the middle of the night, her mother said. Are you all right?

Clare wondered if her father knew how furious she was. How furious she had tried not to be. How furious she would become. Who could ask such a thing of another person? What exactly were the rights of the dying? Were they really so boundless? Would he have asked this of a son? In her experience, men were the ones who tended to become sentimental, hobbled by emotion, while women possessed a certain brutal efficiency. That was why the Final Girl lived—the killer routinely underestimated her ruthlessness. Maybe, because he knew his daughter as well as any other person on earth, her father had anticipated her rage. Maybe he was counting on it.

She said, I'm sorry for waking you.

She said, How's Dad?

n Havana, the festival was in its final days. At the Third Hotel, Isa was on duty at the front desk, no carnation behind her ear, and in a good mood because some girls from Barcelona had left behind recent issues of *Seventeen*. Clare noticed that *The Two Faces of January* had been added to the book collections left out for guests: guidebooks, for the most part, but also mass-market paperbacks, a volume on ancient Rome, a book of poems.

I finished that novel, Isa said. All the people were awful. And there was no detective.

The worst, Clare agreed, as though she knew.

After several inquiries, Clare learned the lone ostrich remained on the loose and that the sightings had continued to abound. The ostrich had been spotted by the Russian embassy. There had even been one report that the ostrich had somehow managed to cross the port of Havana and turn up in Regla.

The flights to New York were booked for the next seventy-two hours. She would see the festival through to the end.

She attended the closing gala at Cine Charlie Chaplin, where the festival director, a heavy man in black glasses and a chocolate suit, made brief remarks about how film was a medium that existed outside the constraints of time—it could see into the future, and it could preserve the past. A Coral Prize was presented to a movie about the early days of the revolution, with a fawning depiction of a young Castro. *Revolución Zombi*, meanwhile, claimed the Audience Prize. From a seat in the back of the theater, Clare watched Yuniel Mata take the stage with his producers; she spotted the director's skirtsuited assistant in the shadows, hovering near the wings. The men embraced, turned to the audience and waved. Next they were bound for festivals in Canada and Spain and France. The gala ended with the screening of a documentary about the formation of the Escuela Internacional de Cine y TV, with the preservation of the past.

At the festival hotel, she could see the strain all the festivalgoers had caused. The kitchen was reportedly out of bread, the bar out of ice. In order to have enough pesos to get to the airport, Clare avoided the drink menu. On her way to the bathroom, she could have sworn she saw Agata Alonso again, in that same black wig—darting around a corner and down a hallway, haloed for an instant in light.

Outside Clare spotted Arlo smoking a cigarette on the edge of the circular driveway, his back to the sloped walkway that led down to the tunnels, in a T-shirt printed with the festival logo, the laminated badge still beating softly against his chest. People poured from the hotel entrance, toward the vintage cars idling on the curb, toward the fleet of yellow taxis waiting out in the streets, dispersing into the night. She wondered how Arlo felt, now that the festival had ended. She was about to walk over and ask him when he flicked his cigarette into a bush and slipped down the walkway, moving with the swift stealth of a person with a secret.

Lights from the hotel illuminated the path; lights embedded in the plants cast a midnight sheen on the leaves. She watched Arlo take his cell phone from his pocket and train the camera lens on the lights; she watched the rise and fall of his slender arm.

Halfway down the path he stopped and turned the camera on himself. Clare hovered in the shadow of a palm tree. In the distance, she could make out the dark mass of the tunnel gate. Was he taking photos? Filming?

She stepped back into the bushes, rustling the branches, and Arlo's eyes snapped up from his phone.

Hey, she said, trying to sound casual and not like a creep.

He took a step closer. He told her to stay where she was and spun the phone around, trapping her in the lens.

Say something, he said.

There was no trace of familiarity in his voice. Her shorn hair and the night had turned her back into a stranger.

I chased a ghost into the mountains, she could have said. I made the ghost and then I drowned him or maybe he was a real man after all, a stranger I let into my bed and then frightened away. It was hard to say what exactly had happened.

Or, It's Clare. Clare with a shitty haircut.

Or, Here we are in the present tense.

She cleared her throat. She touched her skull.

I'm leaving tomorrow, she told him.

You and everyone else.

Arlo pocketed his phone and walked briskly up the path, straight past her. From the top of the walkway she watched him join a small group of people with festival T-shirts. He bummed a cigarette; he tipped his head back and exhaled into the sky, laughing and loose, like he had been among them all along.

On the street a woman on a skateboard shot out of the shadows, sliding to a stop at the mouth of the circular driveway. A taxi driver whistled. Arlo's sister carried a black backpack on each shoulder, her fingers hooked under the straps. She called his name. Arlo put out his cigarette and walked down the sloped driveway, turning once to wave at the group he was leaving behind. When he reached his sister, she gave him a quick kiss on the cheek and handed him one of the backpacks. He took off his festival badge and hung it around her neck. She stepped off the skateboard and tucked it under her arm. They crossed the road and went down an unlit street, backpacks heavy on their shoulders, looking almost as though they were leaving for a trip.

The next day Clare checked out of the Third Hotel for good, and at the airport, from a hard orange chair in the departures terminal, she looked up and glimpsed Agata Alonso in the Plexiglas-walled VIP lounge, one level above the gate area. She wondered if the actress was flying back to Spain, or leaving for some other destination. She was drinking a beer, an arm draped across her stomach, and staring straight ahead. At a TV screen, perhaps. *Hello*, Clare imagined saying to her, in her very best Spanish. *I am a great admirer of what you are doing.*

A woman sat down next to Clare. She wore a plaid dress and leather sandals, her dark hair tied back in a French braid. She asked Clare if she was traveling alone.

Yes, Clare said. You?

The woman nodded. She was in the hotel business and had been in Havana for a week, to inspect a new property. She was from Argentina but lived in Italy now. She had noticed many women traveling alone in Havana, but they were all very young. University students, she assumed.

But *you* are not a university student. She pointed a manicured finger at Clare.

That's for sure, Clare replied.

The woman sighed and said that she dreamed of lying very still on a beach and feeling her mind empty, one thought at a time. Given her line of work, she was unable to enter a hotel without scrutinizing every detail.

The stiller I get the more thoughts I have, Clare did not say.

I know what you mean, she said instead. I'm the same way about elevators.

Work or pleasure? the woman asked, stretching her arms over her head. She stared at Clare for a moment then snapped her fingers.

I'm going with pleasure, she said. I can tell you've spent a lot of time in the sun. Whereas I spent so much time indoors I thought I would turn into a vampire.

The woman's flight was called. When Clare looked back up at the VIP lounge, Agata Alonso was gone.

As they flew away from Havana, turbulence batted the plane around and Clare sank deep in her seat and remembered the quake of the train as it peeled away from the steel path. The world had gone completely silent for an instant, and then that silence was split like a knife through a melon. In New York she would search the Web for more information about the derailment and on a blog she would come across a video recorded on a cell phone, twenty-three seconds of footage. She would watch the lens pass over the slain steel body of the train, the passengers waiting in the grass. She would have to watch five times before she glimpsed two men arguing, heard the child wailing in the background, saw a different child doing a hand-stand, saw three women standing with their arms around each other, saw a lone woman sitting on the ground, face to her knees. For an instant, Clare would mistake this person for herself.

At her laptop, she would think back to *Revolución Zombi*, the hero's plan to record the zombie apocalypse and put it up for sale, about all the curious worlds that would have been exposed in the background, all the unseen corners pulled into the light. When a person did not know they were being watched, what they would do when they believed themselves to be in a state of true privacy—that was the lure of found footage, that clarification of human mystery, and that was why surveillance was so lethal: a true erosion of privacy inevitably led to an erosion of self.

In the footage of the crash, Clare would be invisible, hard to believe she had been there at all.

That would not be the only video Clare would uncover online.

The second would last six minutes, and from the volume of comments and shares, it seemed to be finding quite the audience. The footage would show Agata Alonso kneeling on a concrete floor in some kind of warehouse, in cutoff shorts and a tight white T-shirt and black boots, the treaded soles clumped with mud. The round faces of lights on stands and cameras on tripods peered down like spectators; she was surrounded. A man in khaki shorts and a rumpled linen shirt was standing over her, holding out a blue plastic bucket and bellowing at her to drink. The actress was slumped over, her neck bent. She shook her head again and again. She cried out, shoved the bucket away; a small wave of red rose over the plastic edge and sloshed down on the floor, bloodying her shorts. No one was coming to help her.

In the next shot, this producer stood in the lobby of the festival hotel. People were crowding around him, glasses raised. They were offering congratulations; it was the night *Revolución Zombi* had won the Audience Prize. *Grazie, grazie*, the producer kept saying, raising the trophy over his head.

Next the producer trailed Yuniel Mata's skirtsuited assistant down a marble hallway, a hand planted on her ass.

At the end, Agata Alonso had placed a single credit: her name under DIRECTED BY.

On the flight to Miami, something in the atmosphere of Clare shifted. She did not board her connection to New York. Instead she rented a car and drove north, past Hollywood and Fort Lauderdale and Jupiter. She accelerated toward the source. By Daytona a fat pink moon had started to reveal itself in the sky. It was a troubled moon, she decided. It looked like a looming grievance; it looked lit from within.

She had been gone for more than two weeks and had not sent so much as an e-mail to her boss. On the road, she checked her voicemail and learned that she was no longer an employee of ThyssenKrupp.

On the highway she passed signs for the Matanzas State Forest, and she remembered that in the 1700s the British had traded Havana to the Spanish, who had lost control of the capital during the Seven Years' War, in exchange for Florida—an entire state for a single city.

She reached the Seahorse at dusk, headlights blazing. The parking lot had been expanded, the attached apartment bulldozed and replaced with a swimming pool, a creepy crawler prowling the concrete bowl. The pool was ringed with reclining beach chairs, each with a white towel folded at the foot. Clare was separated from the pool by a plastic fence, a pair of ponytail palms stationed on either side of the gate, which required a code for entry. The panels were bright white, as though they had just been cleaned. The Seahorse was fifty miles from Georgia, the climate less densely tropical than in other parts of the state, the air sharp with salt and chill. She was running her hands over the plastic fence when a woman stepped outside.

The pool is for guests only, the woman called out, her hands flapping.

Clare walked toward the woman, slowly. She wore a striped T-shirt dress and flip-flops, her hair wrapped in a yellow bandana; she looked young, perhaps close to the age Clare's mother had been when they all moved south from the barrier islands. Clare was still holding the car keys; the moon was darkening into crimson. She did not yet know what she was going to do.

I would like to be a guest, she heard herself say.

It was three days before Christmas; there had been a last-minute cancellation. At reception, her mother's fern collection had been replaced by a pair of white orchids, one on each end of the curved desk.

Do you live here? Clare asked as the woman created her reservation. She wore tan braces on her wrists. No name tag.

In Jacksonville Beach? She paused her typing, though she did not look up. The perfect arch of her brows made Clare think of Davi.

No, Clare said. At the Seahorse.

Sometimes it feels that way.

Clare didn't say anything back. Finally the woman looked up. I'm off at midnight, she said. I live in Lakeside.

She went on to tell Clare that she was glad she didn't work the overnight, because those were always the people who got fired. Too many long stretches of aloneness and quiet; it became easy to forget you were being watched. One employee had been caught masturbating, though he claimed to have been sleepwalking and was therefore not responsible; another had been caught making prank calls. The woman pointed to a ceiling corner. Clare turned around and saw a small security camera staring back.

Did you get into an accident? Clare asked, pointing at the braces on her wrists.

The mob got me, she said.

I'm sorry?

Kidding! The woman slipped a key card into an envelope. I have carpel tunnel. I'm writing an epic novel, and it's hell on the joints.

She had the look of someone who had spent a lot of time in physical discomfort: a certain tightness in the jaw, a pinch in the shoulders. Clare asked her what she thought she might get caught doing, if she had to work the overnights.

I don't want to know, the woman said back.

The hallways were still open-air. The walls had been stripped of the cobalt floral wallpaper and painted a tasteful beige. The carpet had been replaced, and the comforter was different too, patterned with red hibiscuses as opposed to lemons and tangerines. The hibiscuses gave the entire room a little too much flush, like over-rouged cheeks. She checked the corners for dead wasps, which more than one TripAdvisor reviewer had complained about, and found none. She counted some small updates in the bathroom: the faucet, the showerhead. The blow-dryer was a different model. Her parents lived not ten miles away and she wondered if they ever came back to witness this particular evidence of time passing.

On the bedside table, the phone rang twice and then went silent.

She set her bags on one of the double beds. She stared at the blank TV. The air in the room felt as still as a freshly departed body, though it was a myth that a dead body was still. Enzymes were digesting membranes; blood cells were sinking into capillaries like tiny deflated rafts, remaking the color of the skin; soft tissues were transforming into gases. She tried to lie down on the unoccupied double bed and on the floor and in the bathtub. She went searching for fingernails and found a business card for a scuba-diving outfit and ate it like a goat.

She looked out the window. The parking lot was illuminated, a curious light cast down from the sky.

In the last months of her father's life, his worst hours would come at nightfall. He would point at a blank wall and cower. He would say that people were living behind the plaster and soon they would be coming to take him away. By then she had moved in with her parents, where she planned to stay until the end. On occasion, she would lock herself in the bathroom and turn on the shower and open her father's notebook. Each time, she felt a blast of volcanic air so dense she thought the molecules were going to arrange themselves into hands and strangle her. Each time, she read a little bit more. *You were an off-putting child, to strangers. At the inn guests always seemed startled to see you. I remember this one couple who called you Little Miss Ghost.* She taped Ellis Martin's card to the back of the notebook. She practiced dialing the number. She knew he would have wanted her to activate his plan—the plan he would now have no memory of—months ago.

She did not take a single photo during these months. She was terrified of what she might see.

Clare and her father would watch TV through the night; it was the only thing that helped him calm. She would rub the parched skin on his hands, examine the blue branches of artery and vein, the Bobtails asleep in a ring around them. Did the cats know? She trimmed his fingernails. She hated it when her own nails inched past the quick; it made her feel as though her whole life was growing out of order. She read an article about suicide tourism. She read an article about Patricia Highsmith and learned she was an alcoholic who brought pet snails to parties. She copied a few quotes into an e-mail and sent it to the Third Hotel, Isa's name in the subject line, knowing it could take days to reach her. She considered what her simultaneous possibilities might be up to—one had walked out into the night and never returned, forged a different path into the unforgivable; in another, her father was already dead.

She told herself anything was possible in the present tense.

She would smell his soggy tartness, the scent of a soul in decline. If a horror movie was on TV, she skipped right over it, because watching someone die slowly—and at the same time all too quickly—beside you was horror enough.

Sports, he would say, and she would go to sports.

News, he would say a little while later, and she would go there.

Sports, he would say, and she would go back.

Where you have been? he would say, and she would tell him, Right here.

No, where you have *been*? he would say.

I have worked very hard at being nowhere and now I'm right here.

Sports, he would say, and she was already there.

Outside the moon had turned gold and red and enormous. It looked like a freshly born planet; it looked like it was sinking down to earth, like it would soon be close enough to touch. A wind roughed up palm trees, pushed a lost sheet of paper across the parking lot. As she passed the reception office, she glimpsed through a window the woman watching a Christmas parade on a small TV and filing her nails.

Clare crossed the road, in the direction of the ocean. You had to be careful at this crossing. No traffic lights, and the cars blew by at blistering speeds, having seemingly sprung from nowhere. As a child, she had once almost been hit by a car. On the opposite side of the road, she turned to look at the Seahorse; the pool gleamed like a gemstone. She felt like her heart was outside her body, beating just above her head.

By the Atlantic the moon was even more monstrous: crimson and swollen and aching with power. A sharp wind stirred the sand. The waves crashed. A cold spray blasted her skin. She watched the darkness spread out before her; she thought of the hero standing at the tunnel gate. The night air set a fire in her throat. She took off down the dark beach. She ran and she screamed.

In New Scotland, in the first days of the new year, Clare would take the reel to a film specialist at the university, a bespectacled man in a sweater vest. When he asked how the water damage had occurred, she would remember hoisting the backpack over her head in the river and she would say, There was an accident. She would not tell him that her husband had used the cinematic condition to investigate her, to build a case. She would not tell him that this was the body of evidence he had gathered and she wanted a verdict. The specialist would require her to leave the reel, so he could attempt to scan the frames. A week would pass. She would meet once more with Detectives Winter and Hall, who would tell her that all forensic evidence suggested the hit-and-run had been an accident. They had made no progress on finding the driver, however. In this way, the case was both solved and unsolved, settled and ongoing.

Nothing is settled, she would want to tell them. Everything is still ongoing.

When she met with the specialist again, he would tell her that the film was unrecoverable: the water had made the base separate from the emulsion; the images were fatally degraded. This man had known Richard and after he said the word "fatally" aloud, he took off his glasses and rubbed his eyes. He would refer Clare to an expert in Manhattan, and that person would offer the same prognosis. Apparently her attempt to dry the film had only made matters worse.

Once something is underwater it should stay there, the second specialist would say.

One night Clare tried to answer her father's question—where have you been? She talked softly as the TV played. She felt as though her blood had been replaced by static electricity. *By the time I stop*, she told herself, *a decision will have been made.* She would not know how to begin, there was no way to begin, but she would begin, she had to begin, and when she did she would have no patience for chronology, for putting things in order, and so she would start at the end or at the beginning, with her return to the Seahorse and the thrashing ocean and the moon, my god, the moon. She would say that she hoped to never see a moon like that again—oh, it had been an evil thing in the sky. When her father blinked and asked his daughter to describe this moon, this evil moon, she would take his hands and the air around her would vibrate, and she would go quiet for a moment because he was listening, he was right here, and she knew this was the last time such a miracle might ever occur.

That night the moon looked like it was going to kill them all.

RESEARCH NOTES AND ACKNOWLEDGMENTS

Revolución Zombi was inspired by the film *Juan de los Muertos*, directed by Alejandro Brugués and considered by many to be Cuba's first nonanimated horror movie (for animated horror, check out the excellent *¡Vampiros en La Habana!*). Aspects of *Revolución Zombi* loosely follow the premise of *Juan de los Muertos*; other details have been invented. The cast and crew of *Revolución Zombi* are wholly fictional and are not in any way intended to resemble the living artists who brought *Juan de los Muertos* to the screen.

During my work on *The Third Hotel*, I turned to a number of texts, many of which left their mark on my own pages: *Cuban Cinema*, by Michael Chanan; *Men, Women, and Chain Saws*, by Carol J. Clover; *Tell My Horse*, by Zora Neale Hurston; *Zombies: A Cultural History*, by Roger Luckhurst; *Projected Fears: Horror Films and American Culture*, by Kendall R. Phillips; *The Dread of Difference: Gender and the Horror Film*, ed. Barry Keith Grant; *American Horrors: Essays on the Modern American Horror Film*, ed. Gregory A. Walker; *Gender and Sexuality in Latin American Horror Cinema*, by Gustavo Subero; *Cuba from Columbus to Castro*, by Jaime Suchlicki; *The Other Side of Paradise: Life in the New Cuba*, by Julia Cooke; *Havana*, by Mark Kurlansky; *Married to the Mouse*, by Richard Foglesong; *Women and Tourism: Invisible Hosts, Invisible Guests*, by Mary Fillmore; *¡Cubanísimo! The Vintage Book of Contemporary Cuban Literature*, ed. Cristina García; *Hotel*, by Joanna Walsh; *Ways of Seeing*, by John Berger; "Examining the

Norse Mythology and the Archetype of Odin: The Inception of Grand Tour," by Maximiliano E. Korstanje (*Tourism: An Interdisciplinary Journal* 60, no. 4, December 2012); "Mapping Urban Horror," ed. Zachary Price (*Mediapolis: A Journal of Cities and Culture*, March 7, 2016); and *A Planet for Rent*, by Yoss. The mention of the *2 +2 =5* graffiti signature is a reference to the artist Fabian Lopez. The Gerry Canavan quote comes from "Fighting a War You've Already Lost: Zombies and Zombis in *Firefly/Serenity* and *Dollhouse*" (*Science Fiction Film and Television* 4, no. 2, Autumn 2011: 173–203); The film description on pages 77–78 is from *Les Revenants*. I'm also grateful to Paloma Duong's scholarship, in particular her lecture "The Commodification of Culture and the Cultural Life of Commodities in the New Cuba," delivered at the David Rockefeller Center for Latin American Studies at Harvard, where I first encountered the idea of screens as "vehicles for the subjective." This novel also found early inspiration in Jean Echenoz's novel *Piano* and Julio Cortázar's short story "Blow Up."

I'm grateful to the MacDowell Colony, Ledig House, Bard College, and the Writers' Room of Boston for the space and time. Thank you to Larry Rohter for the early reading suggestions. Thank you to everyone I met in Havana for their generosity, time, and conversation. Thank you to Shuchi Saraswat for the writing dates. Thank you to Garth Greenwell for the early support. Thank you to Elliott Holt, Lauren Groff, and Mike Scalise for their editorial guidance and encouragement. Mike, extra thanks for the title.

All my thanks to Chloe Texier-Rose, Sarah Scire, Sarahmay Wilkinson, Jackson Howard, Debra Helfand, Rachel Weinick, Frieda Duggan, Abby Kagan, Amber Hoover, and Devon Mazzone at FSG. And thank you to Sarah Gerton and Olivia Simkins at Curtis Brown. It is a privilege to work with all of you.

Emily Bell and Katherine Fausset—you two are the dream team that makes everything possible. Thank you to infinity and back.

Thank you to my family.

Thank you to Paul—for everything, always.